D0968806

Aldo's Fantastical
MOVIE PALACE

Other books by Jonathan Friesen:

The Last Martin

Aldo's
Fantastical
MOVIE PALACE

JONATHAN FRIESEN

ZONDERVAN®

ZONDERVAN.com/
AUTHORTRACKER
follow your favorite authors

ZONDERVAN

Aldo's Fantastical Movie Palace
Copyright © 2012 by Jonathan Friesen

This title is also available as a Zondervan ebook.
Visit www.zondervan.com/ebooks.

Requests for information should be addressed to:
Zondervan, *Grand Rapids, Michigan* 49530

CIP information is available: ISBN: 978-0-310-72110-9

Cover illustration: Yuta Onoda
Cover designer: Kristine Nelson
Map illustration: Brian Oesch
Interior design: Greg Johnson/Textbook Perfect

Printed in the United States of America

12 13 14 15 16 /DCI/ 20 19 18 17 16 15 14 13 12 11 10 9 8 7 6 5 4 3 2 1

To Emma, my hero.

1

"I'M A GENIUS, CHLOE." Dad raised his fists to the sky. "Someday, a teacher will ask you to name the world's greatest inventor, and your answer will not be Thomas Edison, no siree." He lowered a hand, placed it on his chest, and bowed. "You'll say, 'It's none other than humble Ray Lundeen.'"

Chloe laughed. "Humble?"

"Okay, humble is a stretch. But great? Absolutely." Dad led her around the barn to the daisy field and the rusted horse trailer. He pointed to his head, and then shook his finger at heaven. "Today, I will pull Inky, and her trailer, using magnetism!"

"Magnetism?"

"No more need for expensive hitches. And to prove it, I'll haul your horse to the trailhead using the junker."

Chloe squinted. "We don't even drive the Escort anymore. How are you going to pull the trailer with *that*?"

Dad hooted, threw his baseball cap into the air, and raced across the farmyard.

"You are crazy, Dad," Chloe whispered. *But a good kind of crazy.*

The tiny wagon wheezed and sputtered toward the daisies. Dad turned off the engine and sprang out of the beater, heading straight inside the barn. He reappeared moments later fumbling with a chain connected to a series of metal plates.

"Here." He thrust the mess into Chloe's hands. "My latest invention — patent pending, of course. The Connect-It-All. A farmer's dream." Dad straightened and thumbed his suspenders. They snapped against his strong chest. "Now anything can pull anything. What do you think?"

"I, uh, think it's great if it works."

"Sure it works!" Dad scowled. "How dare you doubt your own father?" He snatched the plates from Chloe's hands then bent over, and soon the Escort was fastened to the trailer.

"Prepare to be amazed. She's strong enough to pull three tons." Dad hopped back in the car. "I'm going to pull the chain taut. Then see that white clamp on top of the bumper? Press 'er down and we're good to go."

Tires spun and the engine revved and the Escort inched forward. The chain tightened and creaked against the weight, and Chloe stepped forward.

The Connect-It-All. You finally invented something that works.

"Now?"

"You bet! Clamp 'er! Your mom's gonna be so proud."

Chloe bent over and pushed. "Dad, this is so — "

Snap.

Chain links whipped across her face, and she fell back onto the dirt.

"Darlin'!" Dad's voice faded. "Sweetie! Can you hear me?"

When Chloe opened her eyes, Dad cradled her head, but his face blurred, as if a thick cloud floated between them.

"Am I okay?" she whispered.

That cloud began to rain.

2

"Hop to, darlin'. It's time to walk Grandpa!"

Chloe let her head thunk against her bedroom door. *I'm fourteen, had the upstairs bedroom since I was eleven, but Dad's never once climbed the stairs.*

"I need to get creatin', Sugar-nut."

"You're calling *me* a nut?" she muttered.

Chloe bit her lip, hard. Why couldn't he talk like a normal dad? No more "Mount ups" or "Giddyaps." *There's not a drop of cowboy blood in him; the man's never left Minnesota.*

"Bean Chunk! You hear me up there?"

"Fine," Chloe said.

Sadness washed over her. Short and quiet — those were the only words she could offer him. She wanted to say more, and maybe she would ... someday.

Chloe dressed and bounded down the steps into the kitchen of the old farmhouse. Mom stood at the stove. Even from the back, she was beautiful. Her hair was black like night was black, her skin smooth and dark.

Dad used to say we looked alike. He doesn't say it anymore.

Chloe stroked the raised, jagged scars that stole all beauty from her face and neck. Each night she begged God to erase the ugly white lines. So far, he hadn't.

Chloe watched as Mom's smooth hand cracked an egg on the counter. The yolk dropped all lazy-like into the fry pan before she glanced over her shoulder and forced a smile.

"The twins are ate and gone. I'm sure up to no good." Mom stared out the window where morning haze had all but burned away over the Snake River valley. "It's going to be a hot one today." She exhaled slowly and shook her head. "Hot and sunny and beautiful."

Most people were happy when the weather was nice. But not Mom. Sunny, late-summer days meant kids bought wristbands and filled the pool in Melmanie, instead of buying tickets to fill the seats of Aldo's Movie Palace, the theater she owned.

"Yeah, rotten weather," Chloe said. "Maybe it'll rain tomorrow."

Mom peeled bacon strips and laid them beside the eggs. They crackled and shriveled in their greasy bath. "You're unusually optimistic." She kissed Chloe's forehead and swatted her backside. "Now hurry up. Breakfast is almost ready and Grandpa's waiting."

Chloe scampered out the front door and sprinted to the barn. The doors were shut, but she heard Dad's laugh, his and all the husky-voiced men. Dad's "employees." He paid them with sleeping space in the barn and seats at one of two picnic tables in the Lundeen dining room.

Mom smiled and called them riffraff. "Proof of your father's kindness and goodness." Chloe called them hungry drifters who made Mom work twice as hard.

Chloe tried to ignore them — to keep running, to keep looking left and not peek at the thistle bed that long ago choked out the daisies. But her head turned, like it always did, and there was the horse trailer. And the Escort. And the busted chain. Her feet grew heavy.

"When we're done building the wings — " Dad stepped out of the barn. His gaze bounced from his daughter to the thistles, then to the ground.

"I'm fixin' to rid us of that contraption real soon." His voice softened. "Real soon, sweetie."

Chloe nodded and ran away from the barn, from him, from his promise.

• • •

She reached Grandpa's trailer home, parked in the field between the hen house and the dairy farm beyond. Slow-moving cows mooed in the distance. They looked like black and white boats floating through a sea of green.

"Grandpa?" She pounded on the door. "Grandpa, you ready?"

"In back."

Chloe walked around to the other side of the trailer. Grandpa Salvador was painting again.

He finished with a flourish and stepped back, squinting at his work.

"What do you think, Chloe?"

She stepped back too. "I think you just painted melting fish erupting out of a volcano all around your new ... really obnoxious, bright-blue window."

"Yes, yes. I did. It's a wonder my bad heart was up to it." He winked and tousled her hair. "What do you think about my paving stones? Do they remind you of anything?"

Chloe scanned the row of decorative rocks, painted blue and waiting to dry in the morning sun. "It's like they're from the *Wizard of Oz* ... except they're not yellow."

"Ahaa! This is correct. They are blue! And very difficult to paint. My father would have been proud of me. How I miss dear Aldo, but ..." He grabbed Chloe's hand. "You have come to walk your poor, weak grandpa. Let's put on a good show."

She shook her head and smiled as he dropped the paintbrush.

"Now walk very near today, and keep your arm in mine. I will lean on you from time to time, especially as we pass the house."

"I'm ready." They snuggled close and shuffled across the center of the farmyard. The porch door slammed and Mom stepped out. She shook her head, smiled, and waved.

"Lift my arm and return the gesture."

Chloe did. Mom wiped her eye with her apron.

Together, they made their way onto the path that cut through the fifty-acre field. Only their shoulders and heads would be visible from the house above the wild wheat and hay. Grandpa pulled free and stretched. "Will you go to the pool today? I've heard some swimmers practice before trying out for the swim team."

"Maybe tonight. After … after the kids are gone. But I've been thinking I won't go out for swimming this year."

"Ah, yes. The other swimmers frighten you."

"They don't scare me," Chloe said. "I could beat them all, it's just …"

Grandpa peeked down. "Because in your swimsuit a certain mark is more noticeable?"

Chloe rolled her eyes, and frowned. "Do we have to talk about this?"

"No, my dear, we don't. We can continue to ignore what you continue to run from—"

"Who says I'm running—"

In the distance, they heard a shout, and then a laugh, followed by a string of words Mom would never allow.

"That was Mr. Henks's yell." Chloe stared at the dairy farmer's herd.

"And that was Grif's laugh." Grandpa sighed. "Again, your brothers are up to foolishness."

From the far end of the field they appeared — tall, lanky Grif and short, pudgy Quenton — bounding toward home, paint guns in hand.

"It looks like I'm not the only one painting this

morning." Grandpa pointed at a cow splotched with green. "While it's nice to see they've inherited Aldo's creativity, I have no desire to explain this to our neighbor right now. Come." He picked up the pace.

Chloe glanced from the cows to Grandpa's step. "You look strong today. Why did you pretend?"

"When I'm weak, your mom feels good and needed. She won't feel this way tonight — it will be a slow day at the Movie Palace." He gestured around. "Sunny day and all."

They walked quietly for a long time.

"Do you think my painting will help the green cows erupt with more milk?"

Chloe nodded. "Absolutely."

"Yes. This is what I thought." Grandpa plucked a piece of wheat and put it in his mouth. He chewed and rubbed his stubble and chewed some more. "I lie in bed sometimes and wonder what Aldo would paint if he were here."

Chloe plucked a stalk of hay. "You were lucky to get along with your dad."

"No." Grandpa spit out his wheat. "There was no luck to it. Aldo was stubborn and demanding, and living with him was hard work." He stopped.

"He never called you Sugar-nut." Chloe kicked at the grass and pounded on ahead.

They reached the end of the trail and Chloe slowed. Grandpa caught up and leaned on her shoulder. "Take me to my volcano ... Sugar-nut."

She tried not to laugh, but a giggle squeezed out.

"So you aren't really angry about the name." Grandpa smiled.

They stopped in front of the trailer door, and he stroked Chloe's cheek, traced the scars down her neck, up her chin, and across her upper lip.

"My Chloe. You are beautiful." He gazed over her head. "As beautiful as a distant memory. Young folks do not know how lovely memories are. Without them, what are we?" Grandpa looked back to her. "With them, we are beautiful, as are you."

She couldn't answer, because like their show for Mom, she knew it wasn't the truth. Chloe pulled back from his hand.

"You doubt this?" Grandpa said.

Loud laughter came from the barn, and he continued. "The accident also haunts your father."

"Why can't he talk normal to me? Or even look at me?" She shook her head. "He laughs at Grif and Q and all their ... creativity. I mean, what's the difference between my brothers and me? Only one thing." She pointed at her neck.

Grandpa closed his eyes. Chloe turned toward the house and stormed back passed the barn, where she peeked again.

You sold my horse. Get rid of that trailer.

CHAPTER 3

CHLOE WAS FEEDING CHICKEN SCRATCH to the hens when the brown delivery truck crunched up her driveway.

The truck's tires crackled to a stop. Chloe dropped her sack and Mom dropped her hoe and stepped out of the garden, where she'd been battling weeds. The two stared at each other.

"Hallelujah!" Mom screamed and bolted toward their deliveryman, Mitch.

Chloe laughed and jumped and pumped her fists in the air as Mitch gently laid two canisters on the ground.

"Here!" Mom was out of breath. "Let me sign for these."

Mitch straightened. "So is this going to be a blockbuster?"

"Guaranteed," Chloe said. "Bring your whole family!"

"What movie is it?"

Chloe bent down and stroked the outside of the canisters. "*The Vapor.* Rated R, on six beautiful reels."

She glanced up. Mom gave her the look, and turned to Mitch. "No, this isn't for your young kids. Sometimes Chloe gets a bit excited."

He tongued the inside of his cheek.

"But, Mom, you'll let me see it." Chloe danced around the cans. "Hundreds of times."

Mom rolled her eyes. "You, my dear, are different."

"Nice try, Chloe." He chuckled, climbed back in the truck, and disappeared in a cloud of dust.

"A first-run movie." Chloe shook her head. "How long has it been since we've shown a first-run movie?"

Mom threw back her matted hair. "Too long, and this one cost us dearly. We've a lot to do before it opens tomorrow. Better go in early."

• • •

Mom and Chloe hopped in the work truck with the movie canisters strapped safely between them. Streak, their best mouser, purred in Chloe's lap; her skills were about to be tested. They drove the familiar two miles north toward Fallon and veered left on the Hemming turnoff. Her heart raced, then calmed. Aldo's Movie Palace towered in the distance.

Set on tiny Route 19, and surrounded by nothing but fields and cattle, the theater was Great-Grandpa Aldo's crowning achievement. Nearly eighty years old, the Palace looked nothing like the new theaters with pastel outsides and twenty small screens. Aldo's theater was huge and impressive and built by New York City's finest architects. The Palace was the beginning of another New York City right here in the Midwest.

At least that's what Grandpa Aldo had intended.

Mom eased into the empty parking lot and stared at the marquee.

"I'll start with the sign. Fire up the concessions, and get to work on splicing this together. There are three trailers to add front end and one public service announcement."

"Check."

"Oh, and Chloe ... we have a first-run movie!" Mom high-fived her and hurried out of the truck.

"Streak, it's showtime." Chloe set her down in the parking lot. "I'll meet you inside."

Chloe reached into a canister, extracted the first reel, and carried it up to the projection booth. Five climbs later, sweat dripped off her forehead and coated her fingertips. She grabbed a towel, wiped herself dry, and stared at the two projectors, loaded with this afternoon's feature.

One more day of The Enchanted Island *is about all I can stand.*

Chloe raced down the steps and flicked on the wiener warmer, still loaded with yesterday's hot dogs. She flipped the light switch on the popcorn and popped a kernel into her mouth. And winced.

"We'll definitely need a fresh batch tomorrow."

One hour later, all was ready—Chloe set aside the *The Vapor*, now spliced together on two large projector reels. Her large task done, she bagged the three mice Streak neatly laid out in the foyer and met Mom in the ticket booth.

"We don't have enough ones. We don't have enough fives or tens either." Mom forced a smile. "Never mind. Check the climate of the auditorium, make one last sweep, and then we open."

Chloe carried Streak through Aldo's massive auditorium doors and took a deep breath.

Far above her head, painted storm clouds billowed and spiraled, poking black, spindly fingers across the ceiling. Chloe stared at the strange cloud, and the longer she stared, the more it seemed to spread, to shift. Against the ominous backdrop, friendlier, whiter patches scooted gently across the plaster sky.

"Really freaky, Aldo."

Around the ceiling's edges, three-dimensional planets and moons glowed in front of hidden house lights. They lit up Aldo's wild wall paintings of dripping clocks orbiting skyscrapers in bloom. But even with every light turned on, the room stayed dark, just as Chloe liked it.

The screen didn't.

It seemed to glow with a faint, translucent glow. More than once, Chloe had tried to touch it, only to recoil, her hand tingling and her heart racing. Hands weren't supposed to pass through solid objects. But hers had — right through the screen. Despite what Mom said, Chloe knew.

The screen pit was the one place Chloe didn't dare go.

Welcome to Aldo's magical world, as Grandpa often said.

Chloe sighed. "Nobody can see us in here." She squeezed Streak and walked up and down every row. Mom hadn't missed a single Whopper or Sticky Dot.

"Streak," she whispered. "It's time."

Back in the lobby, Mom wrung her hands. "We okay?"

Chloe nodded.

"So then, we are in competition with what?"

Chloe straightened and prepared for the pre-movie ritual. "Everything."

"What's our objective?"

"Get people in the door."

"Why?"

Chloe smiled. "To sell them junk food."

"Not to see a movie?"

"No, to sell them junk food."

"Because how do we pay the bills?"

"By selling stale wieners and week-old popcorn."

"And so if Mr. Simonsen complains about the price of popcorn today, what will you do?"

"Smile and stand firm." Chloe saluted.

"We're set." Mom retreated into the ticket office. "Lose the cat and get ready to sell."

A half hour later, there was still one truck in the lot.

Chloe leaned over the glass counter and shouted, "Maybe there'll be a late rush! Remember the first day we got *Indiana Jones*?"

"That was a first day. Not a last day."

"Maybe they're all saving up for *The Vapor*!"

"Maybe." Mom stepped into the lobby, raised her arms, and let them flap at her sides. "Maybe they've all just forgotten we're here." She sighed and turned a slow circle. "Maybe we fight a losing battle. It's just there are so many memories locked up in this place." She exhaled, walked over to Chloe, and stroked her hair. "You may as well head on up. I can sure handle it down here."

"Come on, Streak." Chloe climbed into the projection booth and nestled in the chair. She watched the clock above and scanned the seats below. "Nobody, and it's time to start." Chloe paused. "Mom's right. How could we give up on the Palace? All our memories are here." She placed Streak on the ledge. "You might as well keep mousing."

Chloe lowered her out the projection window, flicked the switch on reel one, and dimmed the lights.

"One hour, forty-six minutes, and sixteen seconds of boredom." She exhaled long and loud, reached beneath the splicing table for the mirror, and stared. In the flickering light of the machines, there was only the outline of her face and a few features. But no scars. Not in Aldo's Palace. In the Palace, she was beautiful.

Setting down the mirror, Chloe glanced at the big screen. The actress was beautiful too.

Suddenly, Streak leaped through the window and clawed at Chloe's chest.

"Stop it," she hissed. "I don't need more scratches." She pried the cat loose. "What's gotten into you?"

Below, the auditorium doors creaked.

Customers!

Chloe stretched her neck out the window and peered down.

It was a kid, maybe her age. A slow-walking kid swinging a cane back and forth across the aisle. A kid and a dog. A dog that never left his side.

What's a blind kid doing at a movie?

They eased down to the front row and walked all the way to the end, where the boy lowered himself into a chair. The dog sat in the aisle.

"Don't worry, Streak. I don't think guide dogs ever leave their owners."

Chloe spent the next hour and forty minutes watching the back of a blind boy's head. It swiveled, like he was watching the movie. He looked up toward the clouds and to the side at blooming buildings.

And when the parrot bit the pirate on the ear, he laughed.

Just like he could see.

4

"ONE TICKET," Mom muttered as she locked the theater doors.

Chloe scooped Streak into her arms. "And one hot dog."

"One ticket, one hot dog." Mom sighed. "Do you know what our take was tonight?"

"Five dollars and twenty cents."

"Do you know the expenses we incurred this evening?"

"Second-run movie, last showing — four hundred twenty-eight dollars, give or take."

Mom reached her arm around Chloe and squeezed. "It's lovely. Let's walk home."

The night was cool with no breeze. It was still and silent, except for the scratch of gravel beneath their feet.

Mom said nothing, which was fine — it gave Chloe time to think.

"Mom, that boy who came ..."

"Hmm?"

"He was blind."

"Yes."

"Why did he come?"

"He didn't say." Mom grabbed Chloe's hand and swung her arm. "But his mother and I had a nice talk in the lobby during the movie. They just moved to Hemming from Rochester. Courageous boy."

Chloe kicked at the gravel. "But it doesn't make sense."

Mom took a deep breath of evening air. Around them, frogs and crickets woke up and filled the air with noise, and in the distance a lone coyote howled.

"Some things don't make sense." She drew Chloe close. "You'll give yourself headaches trying to figure it out."

"You sound like Grandpa." Streak leaped down from her arm.

"Good reason for that."

Mom's voice was distant. Chloe knew she'd again entered her worried place, the place where she wondered if she'd be able to keep the theater. Chloe hated it when Mom visited there; she couldn't help but follow her there too.

Their feet crunched onto the drive, and Mom paused. On top of the hill, where their farm stood, red lights flashed.

"Grandpa!" They both broke into a run. Chloe raced ahead, turned the driveway corner, huffed, and stomped to the top. Behind her, Mom ran straight for the sheriff on the porch.

Chloe tried to piece it together. An ambulance sat in front of the hen house. An EMT tried to shoo the chickens away, but the guinea hens had him surrounded and squawked something fierce. Two police cars were parked up near the well, next to the house. Q talked to one officer, while Mom had the sheriff pinned against his squad car, both hands raised. It wasn't easy to calm Mom down.

Chloe forced her legs to move and bolted toward Grandpa's trailer. He stepped out just as she arrived.

"You … You're okay?" she asked.

"I shot your brother." He smiled. "One of my finest shots."

Chloe glanced at Quentin. "Q looks fine."

Grandpa nodded. "Ah, not Q, it was Grif. Yes, filled his buttocks with buckshot."

"You what?"

Grandpa pointed over his shoulder. "Can you see a motorcycle leaning against my trailer?

"Yeah ... Wait, where did you get a motorcycle?"

"That! That is an excellent question. Grif or Q could answer this. They *acquired* it tonight, leaned it against my trailer, and hid in the high grass."

"Wood tick city."

"One can only hope, but let me tell you the story of how I came to hunt your brother. It was late, and Officer Yovich knocked on my door. He asked me if I had purchased a Harley. I told him what I suspected, that Q and Grif were up to no good. He left, and I decided it was a beautiful night for a walk."

"Hey, we walked home too."

"Splendid! So as I walked I heard a coyote. He or she — I do not know the difference — howled very near. I walked on, and again the howl, very near. I think to myself, the situation is worse — it follows me. I sped my walk. The coyote quickened. It rustled at my heels, always out of sight."

Grandpa's eyes grew big. "I broke into the clearing, nearly in a jog. I rounded my trailer, reached beneath the step, and grabbed the gun. Moments later, it rustled again and I shot. It screamed. I thought, this is not the scream of a coyote. It is the scream of a Grif."

"No," Chloe said.

"Yes. And slowly Q stood with his hands in the air."

Behind them, the ambulance lit up and eased away down the lane.

"Now Grif lies on his stomach with lead filling his backside. I'm not pleased I shot your brother, but perhaps it will teach a lesson."

Mom ran up to Grandpa, grabbed his shoulders, and shook.

"What am I supposed to do with you?" She swallowed hard and ran her hands through her hair. "You could have killed him. As it is he'll be scarred — " She winced and stroked Chloe's head. "Sorry, honey."

"Pebble dots on the backside." Grandpa cracked oversized knuckles. "This is true."

"Dad, do you have any idea what happened or what you did or ..." She dropped her gaze. "Anything?"

Grandpa smiled. "Dear Dalia. Yes, I know. And I imagine the story you just heard from Q was convincing in its own creative way, but the night is beautiful, Grif will heal. All is well."

Mom peeked up and looked at Grandpa. Like she wanted to believe him. Like she wanted to think her family and her business were fine. But she shook her head like she couldn't believe it; not when her oldest son was shot by her father, her husband slept in the barn's hayloft, and the only ticket she sold was to a blind boy from Hemming.

Mom threw her hands in the air, spun, and shuffled toward the house. And Chloe's heart sunk with each step.

"Go be with her." Grandpa's hand gently pushed Chloe's back. "Remember, *The Vapor* begins tomorrow and you will be needed. Badly needed. Good night, Chloe."

"Good night back!"

Chloe scooped Streak up from the flowerbed and followed Mom into the kitchen. Her brother was leaned over, his head in the fridge.

"Q!" Mom pounded on the picnic table.

He jumped and smashed his head on the freezer door. "What did I do?"

"*Si sieda!* Now!"

He rubbed his head and eased down onto the bench. "It wasn't my idea. I'm telling you the truth."

"*Now* you tell me the truth?"

Chloe snuck by Mom's angry words and out onto the back porch. She turned the swing, faced it toward the screen door, and plopped down. Through the mesh she could watch the event from a distance.

Mom's silhouette jabbed a finger and flailed a hand above her head. Her words came out loud and fast and slipped in and out of Italian, while Q stuttered in a language Chloe'd not heard before. It looked and sounded just like the final scene from a recent feature, *The Last Trial.*

"Sit right there, Streak. Right by my side." Chloe set her down and closed her eyes. "You can be the world's first guide cat."

She tried to imagine blind; a dark that would never go. She cracked an eyelid — just to be sure the eyes still worked — and then squeezed them tight again.

"And what were you planning to do with the motorcycle?"

Chloe bit her lip and focused on Mom's voice, but it muddled; the cricket song was too loud. She peeked down. No cat. She sighed and leaned back in the swing.

Night always felt good and safe. Being alone felt safe too. But school would soon be here, and that meant kids with staring eyes and the nickname she couldn't bear. She wondered if they'd stare at the blind kid too.

It doesn't matter. At least he won't know.

CHAPTER

5

"Each year is a new start."
Grandpa stomped on the paint can lid, and a drop of white spattered onto his chin. "Look, Chloe." He pointed at his wrinkled face. "Aldo would be proud. Even he never thought of using his face as a canvas."

"I think you should stick to painting your trailer home." Chloe glanced around the farmyard, quiet and still on the first day of school. She grabbed Grandpa's arm and glared at his watch. "Fifteen minutes until the bus comes. Why do I have to go? I don't want to hear that nickname—"

He lifted a finger to her lips. "I don't think your classmates will call you Sugar-nut."

"That's not what they say."

"What do they say?"

Her stomach fluttered. She would not repeat it. Ever. "I, uh — I need to grab my backpack and get to the bus stop."

"Then go." Grandpa stroked her head. "And remember, your grandpa Salvador wishes you the most wonderful of days."

Chloe cleared her throat and ran toward the house.

Most wonderful of days. Most wonderful of days...

She jumped up the steps and burst through the screen door. Clinking forks fell silent. Mom and Dad and five men she didn't know sat around the picnic tables.

Mom rose, grabbed Chloe's face between her hands, and squeezed. "My Chloe. Bella. Now in your first year of secondary school." Chloe pulled back and grabbed her backpack off the table.

"Just think," Mom said. "You and the twins in the same building again."

She didn't want to think about that. Or the bus ride. Or her classmates. Or staring eyes or whispering lips. She wished she could turn off her brain.

"Well, I'm late for the stop. Gotta go."

Mom slapped Dad on the shoulder. He nodded,

his gaze fixed on the table. "Get a move on then, Chloe. I'm right proud of ya."

Mom rolled her eyes and grabbed Chloe by the shoulders, then kissed her on both cheeks. "I'll meet you at the Movie Palace. Four thirty. Don't be late."

Chloe bit her lip, hard.

Only eight hours, forty-one minutes and ... She glanced at the wall clock. *Twenty seconds. Late? Not a chance.*

• • •

Chloe nestled down in her homeroom seat. The bus had been quiet, filled with nervous, sleepy kids. Maybe the nickname disappeared over the summer. More likely, with kids from all three towns sardined into one building, the name got squeezed out. She glanced around the room. Riley and Madison were the only kids Chloe knew, and she'd never heard them speak the word.

Ms. Romero lowered her glasses and glanced over the class. Her gaze reached Chloe's face and stuck. Chloe slumped in her chair and shielded her face with a math book.

The door opened and Chloe straightened. Principal Garret came in first, and a walking stick poked in second. Lastly, a dog and a boy. The blind theater boy.

It was the first time Chloe'd seen him up close. He looked like an average kid. Lots of brown hair and a load of freckles. He wasn't tall or short, he was ... well, normal, except for the eyes. They stared off in strange directions.

His dog was definitely *not* normal. It was a beautiful golden retriever and it stood statue-still at his side. Its tail didn't even wag.

Ms. Romero and Principal Garret spoke softly and whispers filled the room.

"Excuse me, class," Ms. Romero announced. "While I get our new student settled, you can locate your lockers. You have assigned numbers, and you'll find your name taped below them. They're on the opposite wall just outside the door. Go store your things, and to start this year right ... please leave quietly."

The blind boy whispered in her ear.

"Oh, and class. Please do not pet the do —" The kid yanked on Ms. Romero's blouse and whispered again.

The teacher nodded. "Excuse me, this is Hobo. So please do not pet Hobo. He's working."

The class filed out in silence.

Chloe exhaled and reached down for her backpack. Life just got much easier. The blind boy would certainly be the center of attention for a while.

"Ms. Lundeen? Will you please leave the room?"

"Oh, yeah. Sorry."

Locker 245. She double-checked the number printed on her schedule, rose quickly, and scampered out.

The clank of metal and the chatter of students filled the hall. So did words that had nothing to do with her: *blind, dog.*

Grandpa Salvador was right. Each year is a new start!

She walked down the row of bright green lockers, squinting at the tiny numbers. *236, 237 . . .*

Melmanie Secondary wasn't a big school, but it was a green one. Green carpet. Green lockers and green-flecked brick. Chloe hoisted her pack higher on her shoulder and glanced around the forest. Nobody stared back. This was turning out to be the best first day in years.

239, 240 . . .

Up ahead, a laugh. It wasn't the nervous laugh like the ones she'd heard all morning. This was different, and her steps slowed.

241.

A small group of students clumped in front of her.

"Excuse me." She weaved between them.

242, 243 . . .

Chloe froze.

Two girls stopped snickering and stepped back. Chloe moved in front of her locker. Her shiny, new, green locker. The one with 245 on the top and a sheet of paper taped to the front.

She stared at the word, the one scribbled in big letters and with permanent ink.

SCARFACE

Chloe dropped the pack, and her head fell against the locker with a bang. The name found her here, today.

On the most wonderful of days.

CHAPTER

6

CHLOE'S AFTER-SCHOOL BUS rumbled by Aldo's Movie Palace. It used to stop right in front of the theater, but apparently the blind kid sitting in back changed all that. *If only I could get off this bus now.* The steady taunts from the back of the bus had worn thin miles ago.

Bus brakes squealed and the vehicle hissed to a stop.

Oh, wow.

The blind boy's parents must have bought Finnegan's farm, the nicest property in the county. Set on two hundred acres of gorgeous rolling hills, the farm had solid brick outbuildings, two new barns, a horse ring, a pond, and a beautiful view of the Rum River. Not only was it her idea of the perfect house, pleasant memories filled that place. Before Mr. Finnegan died, he gave the locals free sleigh rides along his stream.

Mom said it would sit empty. She said nobody from around here could afford the land, not these days, and since people rarely moved up here that pretty much sealed the deal.

Chloe craned her neck out the window to see over the wrought iron gates. Even in September, Mr. Finnegan's annuals and wildflowers splashed the green lawn with color. *A blind kid's going to miss a lot of beautiful.*

"Nick Harris, isn't it?" Big Tex took his hands off the wheel, peered up into the bus's mirror, and then muscled his body around. "We're at your stop. Welcome to the neighborhood."

The boy shuffled up the aisle, Hobo at his side. He paused at the front seat and turned toward Chloe, as if he could sense her.

"Why do they call you Scarface?"

She slumped down and rolled her eyes. *Even blind kids know that name.*

"Are you mute too?" He waited, shrugged, and stepped toward the door. Tex grabbed his arm, but Nick yanked free. "I can do this myself."

"Easy now," Tex warned. "What with the dog and

the new stop, I was just trying to help. And you need to be okay with that, young man."

Nick eased down the steps, reached gravel, and turned toward the bus.

"You can't help. Nobody here can help."

Tex glanced at Chloe and shrugged. She stood and hoisted her pack onto her shoulder. "Thanks, Tex. You comin' to the theater this weekend? *The Vapor* is a first run."

"You know I don't do that frightening stuff. Stop trying to scare the tar out of me. *Bambi*. Show *Bambi* and I'll be there, front row."

The thought of an ex-marine, tattooed bus driver watching *Bambi* made her smile. She hopped down and the bus pulled away. Neither Nick nor his dog had moved.

"Your house is right there." Chloe pointed, and lowered her hand. *That was dumb.*

"I know where it is," he muttered. "I really want to know about the Scarface thing."

"Well, I want to know about the blind thing."

Nick's brows lowered. "That's none of your business."

"Well, what people call me is none of *your* business."

"Fine, because I don't care anyway."

"Good, because I wouldn't tell you!" Chloe stomped toward the theater.

"Nick! You're back."

Despite herself, she peeked over her shoulder and watched as Nick's mother joined him at the end of the driveway.

"How was the first day? Did you make any friends?"

Nick ripped off his backpack and slammed it down onto the dusty road. "I hate it here. I want to go back to Rochester. Take me home."

Nick's mom hugged him, and he wriggled inside her arms. "Oh, honey, weren't kids kind—"

Nick broke free, fumbled for his pack, and passed through the gate, his voice ringing out extra loud and clear. "I did meet a ... Scarface!"

Chloe stroked her cheek, faced the Palace, and started walking. *Go back to Rochester? What an idiot. Everyone here treated you and that dog like a rock star.*

She stopped and spun. "Well, I met a blind—"

Papers littered the road in front of Nick's gate. The light breeze slowly carried them into the ditch and the bushes and—

"Wait up, Nick! Papers must've slipped out of your backpack."

Chloe raced back to the spreading mess and gathered frantically. *There's like a hundred sheets here!*

She stood, the dog-eared, dusty mess in her hands, and walked toward the gate. "Open up! You left something!"

No answer.

"Great, now I'm a maid for the kid." She straightened the stack. "No page numbers? That's good thinking." She glanced over the top sheet and read.

ON A BROAD, SMOOTH ROAD IN RETINYA …

OFF SET: random shouts and cries

NARRATOR: A strange darkness settles over Retinya, a swirling gray like a coming storm. Nick hears voices, but can no longer see through the evil mass.

THE DARKNESS: How do you like your world now? (The vortex surrounds him.) There's nothing more for you to see. (It continues to billow.) You are mine now.

NICK: (grabs at his eyes) No! I hate you! I hate the darkness!

THE DARKNESS: (its voice softens) You will learn to love me, to serve me, to be me.

Stage directions: The darkness swirls back up into the sky. Nick blinks and falls to his knees. The darkness has stolen his sight.

Chloe leafed through the pages. *A screenplay? You're writing a fantasy screenplay?*

"That's actually kind of cool," she whispered and looked back up through the iron bars. "I'll, um ... I'll keep it safe for you."

She nodded, tucked the stack of papers safely beneath her arm, and walked toward the Movie Palace.

Mom's truck clinked by. She slowed, grinned, and waved. Q saluted her from the back, and Grif, standing, gave his brother's head a whack. No wonder they'd been banned from the bus last year. Chloe shook her head and joined Mom in the lot.

"Well?" Mom opened up her arms.

"I hate it here." Chloe dropped her gaze. "I want to go back to Rochester."

Mom squinted and brushed the hair off Chloe's face.

"Forget it. Just heard the blind kid say it, and it felt about right to me too."

Mom pursed her lips, and Chloe continued. "Same old. Same name."

"If you want to move to Rochester, I'll help you pack," Grif jumped down and winced. "I tell you, that old man started something — "

Mom froze him with a glance.

"Do you know I had to stand in every class like a dunce?"

"About time they put you in the right place. You get one of them dunce caps to wear?" Q grinned.

"Inside, you two. I asked you to help on opening night, not to drive customers away. And Grif, that old man is your grandfather."

Chloe tossed her backpack into the truck and slammed the door.

"Maybe Nick will end up being a friend." Mom unlocked Aldo's and they stepped inside. The dank, cool air enveloped Chloe. Safe at last.

"Doubt it. Nick's worse than the others. He talks short and angry." Chloe stared down at the screenplay. "I just don't think—"

"He's been through a lot." Mom exhaled long and slow. "Don't give up on him."

Whatever. I never started with him.

Chloe cranked the handle of the hot dog heater to activate the motor. "I have enough problems at school. I don't need more."

Mom nodded. "I'm sure you'll figure it all out. I did invite Nick's family to dinner Friday, so try to make nice by then."

Chloe stopped cranking. "You didn't."

"They're new to the neighborhood. You know how your father likes to be hospitable."

"To everyone but me!" Chloe ran up to the

projection room, set down Nick's play, and lifted reel one into place. *What do you think? Should we invite Nick over? Let's ask Chloe how she feels.* "A little courtesy would help around here!"

A cough echoed from the theater seats. Chloe glanced out the window. Mr. Simonsen.

"You all right up there, Chloe?"

"Yeah, sorry." She clicked the reel and dimmed the lights. "Never better."

Dinner with Nick. That's a real horror movie waiting to begin.

She slumped to the floor and Streak jumped onto her lap. "Been waiting for me? Sorry. I've been cleaning up after Nick." Streak licked her front paw. "Don't worry, you don't want to know him."

Chloe peered up at the screenplay, thought for an instant, and reached for the stack. Soon the sheets spread out over the entire projection room floor.

"Streak, there has to be some order to these, but I can't figure it out." She picked up two papers and glanced back and forth. "There's hardly any description of this world. It's all dialogue. Where do these river dwarfs come from? And here, what's a Calainian?"

She held a sheet in front of Streak, who curled up and closed her eyes. "Take these guys who live underground. He calls them Quints. I have no idea what they look like or — " Chloe bit her lip and grabbed a pen off the counter. "Quints. Sounds like Quenton. They'd be short and fat." She scribbled a few lines in the margin.

It's not like he's going to see it.

"And then there are five massive cities. Medahon, Shadowton, the City of Reckoning … and some I can't quite pronounce. No description." She looked out the small window into the expanse of Aldo's Palace. "Let's make Medahon a city Aldo would love."

Chloe scrawled *Notes on Medahon* on the back of a page.

Stairs to the sky, leading nowhere.

Walls, thick, but filled with labyrinth-like tunnels

Beneath Medahon lives an entire race of —

The door to the projection booth flew open, Streak shot off her lap, and Nick stumbled forward, his screenplay crinkling beneath his feet. He released Hobo and turned a complete circle.

"You can't be up here," Chloe hissed.

"Please tell me you have my movie script and please say I'm not standing on it right now."

"You dropped your script, and I was *kind enough*

to save it. As for stepping on it … yeah, you are, but people don't just burst up here, and I was only trying to get the pages in order. What kind of screenplay has no page numbers?"

"What kind of person steals my script?"

"The same type who tried to return it, but the owner was too busy whining to come out and get it!"

"So now you're using it for a rug?"

"Chloe!" Mr. Simonsen hollered. "Hold it down, please."

"Sorry!" Chloe yelled down, still facing Nick. "Here!" For the second time that day she scooped up the papers, this time stuffing them into Nick's hands. "Take your stupid script. I'm so sorry for trying to help you! Why do you carry it anyway? You can't read it."

"Again, none of your business." Nick hugged the script.

"Fine."

"Fine."

Nick spun to leave, and Hobo moved to the front of the open door. "Let's go home, boy."

Chloe pushed her hand through her hair. "Hold it. Okay, I shouldn't have put it on the floor, all right? And I shouldn't have looked through it or … made minor notes in places."

Nick froze. "You made notes."

"I just thought some of your descriptions needed spicing up —"

"If I wanted your help —"

"You'd ask for it. I know. I'm sorry, I just thought —"

Nick walked out, slamming the door behind him.

"Well." Chloe took a seat. "We can continue this delightful conversation over dinner at my place."

• • •

The week at school passed slowly and painfully.

It wasn't much better on the farm.

Dad's over-the-top sense of hospitality turned Nick's visit into a major event, and by Friday cleanup reached fever pitch. Mom even closed Aldo's Palace for a day to help with the straightening.

Chloe finished feeding the animals and cleaning their pens, and stood in the middle of the farmyard.

We are an Italian version of the Addams Family.

Dad mowed the yard with his new invention: the Green Machine. He bragged, "No damage to the environment." And he was right on that point. Of course, two slow-moving cows pulling an old tractor pulling fifteen fainting goats that chewed up grass was mighty hard to control.

"Plus, she don't take an ounce of gasoline. Now, I

admit to an uneven chew — er, cut — but Plum Cake, I think I'm on to somethin'."

Yeah, more public humiliation.

Q snuck cigarettes behind the chicken coop, and yelled "boo" when Dad's contraption passed. All fifteen of those fainting goats toppled to the ground. So did Q, in fits of laughter.

Near the field, Grandpa repainted his home, covering it with blue windows.

"Everybody's losing it." Chloe tongued the inside of her cheek and glanced at the house. On the porch, an angry Grif cleaned his pellet gun, occasionally aiming at Grandpa Salvador's backside, and in the garden Mom fought wet wood to start a bonfire.

Yep, the strangest family in Kanabec County. Good thing Nick won't see any of it.

By late afternoon, all was in order. Which was one reason Chloe dashed outside at the sound of Dad's idling truck. Her brothers hooted and hollered and threw each other against the side of the truck bed.

"Where are you guys going? Dinner is in a few hours!"

"Fishing." Q stepped toward Chloe. "Um. Dad said he wanted a fish fry when your friend comes over." He paused. "You want to go dig some crawlers? He didn't ask you to come, did he."

"When does he ever ask me?" Chloe felt her jaw tighten.

Q exhaled. "It's been a while."

"Hey, Q, get my tackle box!" Grif shoved his brother, who stumbled into Chloe. "Oh, didn't see you there, sis. You might want to make yourself scarce. Dad'll be here soon and it might be awkward, him not wanting you along and all." Grif raised his eyebrows, grinned, and climbed in the cab.

Q looked at Chloe, started to speak, but then closed his mouth.

"Okay, boys, let's mount up and hightail it outta—"

Dad came around the back of the truck and ducked his eyes at Chloe. He breathed deep and removed his cap.

"Reckoned we better catch some fish for your friend," Dad said, and dug his toe in the dirt.

Chloe stepped back and spoke quietly. "I like to fish."

"Don't you worry none." Dad backed away too. "We'll provide a feast."

"I like to fish."

Dad took another deep breath and forced a smile. "Come on, boys. Chloe's countin' on us."

They all hopped in, and the truck pulled away, Q's face pressed against the glass.

"No, Dad. I stopped counting on you long ago."

Chloe raced to Grandpa's, her heart pounding.

"I hate him, Grandpa. I hate …" She burst into tears. It took several minutes, enveloped in Grandpa arms, before her crying slowed.

"I think I would like a date with you. Do you have some time, Chloe?"

"Now?"

"It's not too late. Go get your swimsuit and meet me by the river path. It's been a while since I've gone for a swim."

Chloe sniffed and nodded. When she reached the path, there stood Grandpa Salvador, white wisps fluttering out from beneath a bright orange knit cap.

"It's not hunting season yet." Chloe grinned.

"No, it is not. But this does not seem to stop your brothers. Besides, I think Grif, when he returns, would not think twice about peppering me given the excuse."

He took Chloe's hand and walked down toward the river. The east turned a deep shade of blue while the western sky blazed with pinks and purples.

"Your father does not know what he's missing," Grandpa said.

"He knows. I know. Everyone knows. He's ashamed of me."

"He is many things—"

"Yeah," Chloe interrupted. "Crazy. Cruel. Cuckoo. A lot of *C* words, actually."

Grandpa squeezed her hand. "Your father is many things, but ashamed of you is not one of them." He straightened. "My Chloe, I've come to enjoy our late swims over the years, and yet I can't help thinking you would have more fun at the pool with your friends."

"I have classmates. I don't have friends."

"Hmm. I have a feeling that some are not too far away." Grandpa looked to the clouds. "Do you see those puffs? Your great-grandpa Aldo used to tell me that one day he would figure a way to ride them across the sky. Then he'd take me for a ride. What do you think?"

"I think Aldo was crazy."

"Perhaps." Grandpa swept a clump of grass from the path. "But when I see the sky, I am sure I see him looking down on me. All these years, and I still care what he thinks."

"He thinks you look weird in that hat."

Grandpa removed it and stuffed it over Chloe's ears. "I can't be caught looking weird."

They stomped through the trees that lined the Snake River and stepped down onto the sandy shore.

Chloe relaxed and slipped off her outer clothes, setting the orange hat beside the pile. The cool sand squeezed between her toes and she relaxed. She was near water. She could dive in and disappear.

After Aldo's, the Snake River sand strip was the safest place she knew.

"And what is your goal tonight?" Grandpa asked.

"To reach the Northern Bridge."

"But this is against the flow."

She nodded. "And what is your goal?"

"I will jump into the water and forget. All the problems that feel so large, I will leave on the shore. They will wait for me and be there when I emerge. I will worry about them then, but for a few moments, I will forget." His eyes twinkled. "Will you join me in forgetting? Just for tonight?"

Chloe smiled. A late evening mist hung low, and she checked her entry for rocks and dived into the cool relief. She felt the undertow and began a gentle stroke.

Go ahead and catch fish, Dad. I'll be here, in a world for Grandpa and me.

A splash, and then bubbles everywhere. Chloe surfaced and looked at Grandpa now wearing his orange hat — and only his orange hat. The rest of his clothes were balled up on shore.

"Grandpa!" She laughed.

"It has been too long. Avert your eyes from this wrinkled old man. Swim now!"

And Chloe swam. The last hint of twilight shimmered the water as she reached the bridge. In the distance, headlamps and shouts lit up the driveway. Dad was back.

The end of a perfect night.

7

Nᴏᴏ Hᴀʀʀɪꜱ'ꜱ Sᴜʙᴜʀʙᴀɴ crunched to a stop near the barn.

"Go on, Chloe." Mom pushed her away from the stove. "You should be the one to welcome them."

Chloe's shoulders drooped. "But you don't know Nick."

Mom pointed and Chloe shuffled outside. Little clouds of dust surrounded her work boots and vanished into the air. *Lucky dust clouds.*

The car doors opened and out popped two smiling adults, one surly kid, and a dutiful dog.

"Hi, I'm Chloe. Welcome to our place."

Nick and Hobo brushed past her and marched toward the barn.

Chloe puffed out air, and Mrs. Harris walked over and offered a hug. "You'll have to forgive Nick."

I'll think about it.

"Thank you," she continued.

"For what?"

"For being so kind to Nick. He talks about you all the time."

Chloe glanced at Nick, who, with his dog, stepped inside the barn to do who knows what. "I think you're hugging the wrong kid." She pulled away.

"No, he specifically mentions Chloe Lundeen."

It made no sense. Nick made no sense.

Mr. Harris joined them. "So this is the famous Chloe."

Nick's mother reached under Chloe's chin. "I'm sorry that school is so horrible for you." She lifted Chloe's face. "That bully Scarface should really be disciplined—"

Mrs. Harris's gaze fixed on Chloe's neck, and she lifted her hand to her mouth.

"Yeah." Chloe rolled her eyes. "I'll make sure to report myself to the principal first thing." She raced after Nick.

I won't be joining this dinner party. Tears fell, and Chloe kicked the metal barn doors and didn't care that Mom saw. Chloe pounded inside.

"Nick? Nick! How could you tell your parents — "

"I had Mom read me your notes."

Nick's voice sounded small, the words barely audible from the rear of the barn. He sat on a hay bale in the corner. Had Nick been able to see the wrecking ball Dad used to crush failed experiments now hanging from the rafters, he likely would have made a different seating choice.

Chloe slowed and frowned.

"They're good. They made the script better." Nick shifted. "Not that I couldn't have made it better myself, but they … I was wondering if you …" He squeezed his hands tight. "Do you want to help me with my script?" He stood and pointed in Chloe's direction. "This would be a professional relationship only. We do not have to be friends."

"You're asking me for help?" she said.

"No! Not help. Just … feedback."

"Feedback."

Nick jumped up. "Do you want in or not?"

"And this would not be a friendship, because I pretty much came in here to pound on you."

"Definitely, not a friendship."

Chloe folded her arms. "And if I do this, you agree not to refer to me by the other name. Ever."

"Which name? You mean Scarface?"

"Nick!"

"Just kidding." He grinned. "Yeah, it's a deal."

Nick's grin disappeared and he tilted his head. "I'm standing beneath something heavy, aren't I?"

"Yep. And two feet to your left rests a blowtorch. Behind you on the wall hang five chain saws, three axes, and a maul. His trough filled with shattered glass isn't too far away, either. You're in the workshop of Crazy Ray, aka my dad." Chloe glanced around. "The hayloft is safe."

"Can we go up there?" Nick grasped Hobo's harness tighter.

"Nope. That's where my dad sleeps. I've never been up there." She peeked up. "Well, not since ..."

"Get me out, boy." Nick and Hobo slowly weaved their way out of the barn. Chloe stood and watched them go.

What did I just do? More time with Nick?

The smell of sweet smoke filled the air and in the distance there was laughter. Words, evil words, rode the scent into the barn.

"I'm so sorry, I had no idea that she was the Scarface, or that she'd been hurt until I looked at her."

I hate you, Mrs. Harris.

"Yeah, some people call her Chloe, others call her Scar — that name. She's kind of like two people in one."

I hate you, Nick.

"Had no inkling myself of what my sweet glass of Kool-Aid was going through at school."

I hate you back, Dad.

"Ah, my Chloe. Bella. Bella. Bella. Such a beautiful girl, is she not?"

Grandpa Salvador. You, I love.

"No!" Nick shrieked. And suddenly all voices spoke at once.

"Chloe? *Venite fuori!* Now!" Mom's voice rose. Chloe scampered outside and froze.

Nick lay on his back clutching his head, his body writhing, while his parents knelt at his side. Dad raced back from the house holding cloth, and minutes later, sirens blared.

Time blurred with shouts and cries and lights, as the ambulance made its second visit in two weeks to the farm.

"What are you thinking?"

Chloe jumped up and turned. Grandpa Salvador stood silently at her side.

"You scared me!"

"Yes, it seems I have. What are you thinking?"

She fell back against the metal door and watched as Nick was lifted onto a stretcher and vanished inside the ambulance.

"I'm scared, Grandpa. I feel like I should do something but there's nothing a kid—"

"Oh, I believe you will do far more for him than you could imagine. Remember, don't let him go, Chloe. Don't ever let him go."

Chloe stared at Grandpa. "If everyone else likes him so much, why don't we just adopt him? To me, most times, he's a jerk." She peeked at worried Mr. Harris. "I mean, this isn't what I want, but how am I supposed to endure someone who hurts me each time he opens his mouth?"

"See." Grandpa gestured with his head. "His parents will ride with him. Doctors will too, but perhaps not the dog?"

Chloe glanced at Hobo and thought. "Yeah, I can do that. That dog seems nice." She leaped up and ran toward the ambulance. "I'll watch Hobo!"

"Yes." Nick's mom broke into tears. "Oh, thank you. Here's our gate's code." She dug in her purse for a scrap of paper. "We'll be back for Hobo soon." The back doors silenced her sentence and the sirens wailed into the distance.

"What just happened?" Chloe whispered. "Did he fall?"

Dad took off his baseball cap and scratched his

head. "Don't rightly know, Honeycomb. Something inside the head's not right."

Chloe did know one thing. She had a dog to deal with. But not like any dog she'd had before. He stood statued, staring down the gravel drive. Waiting. He'd probably wait forever if she let him.

"Honey." Mom approached. "You should probably walk Hobo back to Nick's place. I'll let him out in the morning, and you can hop off at the Finnegan property and check on him after school, before coming to Aldo's." Mom wrinkled her forehead at the dog. "I declare, he looks like he blames himself. I think he needs to be in familiar quarters."

Chloe nodded. She wouldn't know what to do with a comatose dog anyway.

Chloe walked silently beside the dog, her hand on the harness. The animal looked lost in thought.

"Excuse me, Hobo. I don't mean to interrupt you, but ... what's wrong with Nick?"

Hobo started to pant.

"Okay. It's been a tough day."

They reached the gate and Chloe punched in the security code. Metal creaked and the door opened inward. Hobo didn't flinch.

"Come on, Hobo." Chloe stepped inside. "Come on, boy."

The wind blew cool, and summer leaves danced down the road behind him, but that dog did not move.

She knelt. "How am I supposed to take care of you if you don't come inside? If you do this on Monday, I'll be late for the Palace. You're a working boy, I'm a working girl. You understand." She paused. "Hey, Nick will be back. He'll be okay."

Hobo looked up, then down, and eased by her and through the gates. Chloe shut them with a clang, jogged by the gardens, and found the hide-a-key.

Once inside their expanded farmhouse, she gasped. The house was beautiful. Not modern beautiful. Olden days beautiful. With chandeliers and antique furniture and pictures of people from long ago.

"Well, Nick. I don't know what your dad does, but he must do it well. Better than my dad, anyway." She turned to Hobo. "Where's your dish? Of course, Nick's room."

It took a bit of exploring to find it. But when Chloe pushed open the last door on the left and turned on the light, she knew she was there. Boy clothes were stacked neatly in piles on the bed. No pictures or posters graced the walls, but in the far corner, stacked in a floor-to-ceiling heap, was the strangest assortment of stuffed animals. Trolls and dragons and wizards. Fantasy stuff.

Chloe filled the dog dish and stood. "I'm guessing the harness stays on you, Hobo? Yes? No? Though if I removed it, I don't think I could get it back on." She took one last look around the room and her eyes widened. *What a computer screen!*

The screen saver was beautiful. Chinese Mountains. Chloe moved nearer.

"Too bad you can't see it."

Too bad you can't see it.

The mountains disappeared and her words typed themselves on the screen.

"What a great app."

What a gate app.

"I said great, not gate."

I said great, not gate.

Chloe sat down, grabbed the mouse, and scrolled up the document.

Page 1
RETINYA
Screenplay by
Nick Harris

"So you added page numbers, huh?" Chloe smiled. "Excellent idea, Nick. However did you think of it?"

Her words appeared on screen and she winced.

He won't want my sentences in there.

She deleted them, hit save, and silently read:

> *"How could you do this?"*
> *"Do what?"*
> *"You know, bring me here. You don't know the Darkness that awaits."*

Pages and pages of dialogue filled the screen. But there was no description. No narrative.

Of course, Nick probably doesn't know, or can't remember, or...

Chloe thought for an instant, leaned in, and spoke.

> *The lake stretched out for miles, clear and blue and shimmering, with clouds of pink and purple ...*

Hobo barked and stared intently at the screen.

"You don't like pink and purple? Fine." She turned back to the screen. "Patches of white hovering over the water."

Chloe kept adding. Hobo kept barking. Finally, Hobo lay down and Chloe glanced at the clock.

"Wow, okay, better get home, but at least it reads a little smoother." She powered down the computer. "I think he'll like it, don't you? I mean, you heard him — he said I could help."

Hobo was asleep. Chloe slipped out of the room, off their property, and ran home.

Weeks passed, and inside Aldo's Movie Palace *The Vapor* was a huge success. Mom smiled a bit more, and seemed to worry about Grandpa a bit less. Who would have thought a horror flick could make such a positive difference?

The kids at Chloe's school continued to be horrid, but her mind was elsewhere — in a different world: one named Retinya. Nick's fantasy was alluring and terrifying and offered the perfect escape. Chloe dreamed of it, sketched out its inhabitants, and spent Mr. Kolberg's algebra class creating detailed maps of the landscape.

"Chloe?"

She carefully traced the Wandering Road, marked the location of the wood elves' invisible kingdom, and stared lazily around her kitchen.

"Chloe!" Mom clanked two pans together.

"Oh. Sorry. This homework is really absorbing."

"Absorbing." Mom frowned. "Maybe my task will bring you back. I want you to take a break from Aldo's. Q will take your place in the booth after school starting today."

Chloe dropped her spoon into her Cheerios. "But we've never done so well. Don't you need me?"

"Someone needs you more." Mom eased down across from her. "Nick's mother called. Apparently, Nick's back home. He won't be in school tomorrow, but he'd like to see you. Something about a screenplay?"

"He wants to see me?"

"That's what Mrs. Harris said. I want you to go over to their house after school."

"But —"

"He's expecting you."

Chloe pushed away her cereal bowl — she wasn't hungry. She'd been making changes to his script every day for two weeks.

This little meeting isn't going to be pleasant.

School zoomed by, and Chloe stepped off the bus in front of Nick's gate, her stomach filled with butterflies. She entered the gate's code, walked up to the door, and knocked.

It swung open immediately.

"Is that you, Chloe?"

"Yeah, Nick. I — Ow! Don't yank the hair!"

With a yank, Chloe's attempt at a pre-war peace talk was ended promptly, and she had no choice but to follow him to his room. Nick sat in front of his computer in stony silence. She stared at the screen and chewed her nails.

"I thought your work here was limited to taking care of Hobo."

"Okay, it was." Chloe took a deep breath. "But Retinya, it's really good. I kind of got lost in it. Blame Hobo too. He helped."

"My dog helped you write a script?"

Hobo turned away.

"It was weird. He barked and I wrote and — Oh, like I've been trying to say, I may have gone too far."

"May have? I listened to the script. I should just call it Re-Chloe-ia." He hinted a smile.

Chloe bit her lip. "You're not mad."

"I was. But then I listened again and, well … you're kind of making it better. I thought maybe you could come over sometime, and we could work on it *together*."

Chloe nodded. "Yeah, I'd like that. I have some ideas for your good guy … Secholit? Is that how you pronounce that? And your bad guy — Darkness — I think we can frighten him up a bit — "

"Whoa." Nick stiffened. "Here are the rules. You don't mess with Secholit. You don't mess with Darkness. Here are the other things you may not change." He handed Chloe a sheet.

She sighed. "Wait. No. Like here. I have great ideas for the Safelands. It's a desert, with sand, like the riverbank behind our place. Sand is always safe 'cause it's near water."

"No! Sand is never safe. You know why? *It's near water!* Try being blind and walking near a river. Not smart. Just like climbing trees. Not smart."

"That's always smart! Nobody can see you up in a tree. Nobody laughs at you. This Unknown Forest? That has to be a good place!"

Nick stood. "This will never work. Chloe, here. Take the original. Make the changes you want, I'll make the changes I want. Then we'll get together tomorrow and fight about it. Fair?" He handed Chloe the dog-eared sheets she knew so well.

"Yeah. I mean, it is your play."

Midnight came, and Chloe was still hard at work. "A wind funnel. Like the tornado that came through last year. A tornado *inside* a mountain." She scribbled in the margin. "How cool would that be?"

Mom knocked and poked in her head. "To bed. I'm sorry, but, Chloe, I need you back at Aldo's. Q tried—he's a good boy without Grif—but he's useless. He showed reel two first."

"He didn't … No, Mom! I really can help Nick. I think he does need me."

"Yes, he does. Unfortunately, I do too. Turn off the light."

Chloe grabbed the papers, stuffed them in her backpack, and drifted off into the Unknown Forest.

• • •

"Nick, I can't come tonight." Chloe plunked down beside him in the lunchroom. "Mom needs me at Aldo's."

His face fell. "Yeah, I get it."

"It's not like I have a choice."

"Sure."

An awkward silence settled over them. "Here are the changes. There are a whole lot of them, some on every page. I'm telling you, this could be incredible!"

"Right."

"Hey, Nick!" A boy called from the table behind them—a voice Chloe did not know. "Did you get blinder? How come you need two guide dogs? A quick FYI, they gave you a scarred one!"

Laughter, ugly and cruel, filled Chloe's ears. "Here," she whispered. "I'll just leave my ideas in front of you."

"Don't go," Nick reached for Chloe's arm, but she'd already stood.

"I can't stay." She turned and walked quickly out of the lunchroom.

There's only one safe place for me.

W HAT DID YOU DO TO MY SCREENPLAY?"
Chloe jumped, and the reel she held slipped
from her fingers. She lunged for it but caught only
the end of the film.

Snap.

Reel one of *The Vapor* saucered to a clattery stop
to the ground. At least the frame of it. She stared at
the coil of film in her hands.

"Oh no. Nick, do you have any idea — Oh no. Do
you think we keep these? Do you know how much
this film cost us?" She dropped to her knees and gently hugged the reel.

"Well, too bad for you. Now, maybe, we're even.
You ruined my movie, I ruined yours."

Chloe stared up. "You can't keep coming up
here — How did I ruin your movie?"

"Mom found your version when I got home from school, and while I was out with Dad, she typed all your changes into my original. It's a whole new script! I mean, I don't recognize the half of it."

"And you're blaming *me* for that?" She peered at the clock. Five minutes to showtime. She stood and looked out the window. Easily one hundred customers. *Of all the days.*

Chloe placed the reel and the piece of snapped, kinked film onto the splicing table. "This will take thirty minutes," she mumbled. "Maybe forty." She swept sweat from her forehead. "Think, Chloe."

"Who cares about that? What about this?"

Nick threw Chloe's draft in her direction. Pages filled the air and fluttered onto the splicing table, covering the movie reel.

"Why are you doing this to me?" Chloe threw up her arms. "Is it your goal to make my life officially misera — ?"

Behind her, the damaged reel rattled beneath the blanket of papers.

"What the — Oh, where's Streak when I need her? Don't suppose that super dog can catch a mouse! I hate mice!" Chloe carefully lifted the sheets, and Grandpa's full mantra floated through her head:

Aldo's Fantastical Movie Palace — where dreams come true, and nightmares too.

"This would qualify as a nightmare," she whispered.

"Chloe!"

Mr. Simonsen!

She stretched her neck out the window. "Movie is coming up. Technical difficulties! You've already seen it seven times, so a little patience ..."

Chloe turned in time to see a wisp of smoke vanish beneath the papers. "Okay, that's bizarre." She swept away Nick's screenplay and gave the table a hard stare. "I don't have time for eye tricks." She jammed the dented first reel onto the projector.

"Oh, God, I need a miracle here. Let the break be during the public service announcement!"

"Hey!" Nick yelled. "That better not be my screenplay I hear getting all crinkled."

"You threw it, you goof."

Click. The preview started.

"And as for you, Nick. Here!" She hissed, punctuating each word by stuffing a paper into his hand. "Once again, I'll pick up your screenplay, and this time I promise I ... won't ... ever ... mess ... with .... your ... dumb ... screenplay ... again."

She braced for his comeback. There was none, and she slumped to the floor.

"Is the movie playing?" Nick whispered.

"Yeah, no thanks to you."

Nick inched toward the clicking reel. "Can I ... can I feel the projector?"

Chloe puffed out air. "Fine." She stood and grabbed his hand and pulled him forward. He stroked the machine, placed his ear and cheek against it.

"Can I look through the lens?"

"You can't —"

"Can I look through the lens?"

Chloe gently pushed his head against the glass viewer in the rear.

"Light." He pulled back, repositioned his eyes, and again pressed forward. "I saw light. Red. Green."

Chloe frowned and stared out the window at the big screen, at the red sky above a field of green. "You're just seeing the opening scenery — Wait, you can see?"

Nick jumped and rocked and rubbed his eyes. "More. I want to see more."

Chloe glanced down the stairs and turned back into the room. "You know, maybe this isn't the time —"

Gone.

Nick and Hobo were gone. Chloe spun around the booth, stared out the window, and gasped.

A boy and his dog walked toward the screen inside the projection beam, hovering above the audience. As if light was solid.

It was Chloe's turn to rub her eyes. None of the customers seemed to notice the small beings above their heads.

"Hello!" she called out. "There's a boy? In the beam? Doesn't that bother any of you?"

She jammed her eyeball against the viewer, felt a sucking sensation, and soon stood blinking inside the blinding light of the beam. "This isn't happening. I must've fallen and smacked my head and turned delusional." Chloe glanced straight down as Little Jim dumped his weakened soda on the floor.

"Hey, knock it off! I have to clean that up!"

Ahead, on the screen, Nick groped about the room, bouncing off screaming children.

He's in the worst scene! He's in the movie!

"Chloe!" Nick screamed.

"Stay put, I'm coming!"

Nick heard her, and froze center left. The other kids vanished from the room, and through the crack beneath the room's door appeared a wispy, grayish hand.

Chloe reached the screen, leaped, and felt the surface give like a trampoline, before it jelloed and sucked her in. Chloe gasped and sprung to a stop beside Nick and Hobo.

"This has never happened before! Why is this happening now?" Chloe saw Mr. Simonsen and the rest of the audience at Aldo's staring at them.

"Hey!" she yelled and waved her arms. "It's us. Get my mom! Turn off the projector!"

Hobo barked, loud and frightened, and a second wispy arm materialized.

The Vapor!

"Nick." Chloe ran to him. "We need to get out of this room."

"Why? The screaming stopped."

Chloe chanced a look at the two arms stretching toward Nick's legs. Hobo bristled and throated a low growl but stood his ground.

"Let's just say I've seen this movie before and this isn't the best scene to be stuck in."

She grabbed Nick and pulled him toward an open window. The Vapor massed inside the doorway, its apelike arms grasping toward them.

"Nick, we need to jump." She raised her head over the sill. "It's about a ten foot drop. Can you do that?

Can Hobo — Wait. This window's bright blue. It's never been blue before."

"Blue? A blue window? That's my way in. I wrote that! Follow me."

Nick felt his way forward. The mist gained, nipped at his heels. Nick stumbled, landed hard on the sill and scrambled through.

"Nick!" Chloe screamed.

The Vapor roared, gathered itself, and moved toward Chloe. Its fingers climbed up her legs, which fell numb at the touch. Falling to the ground, she dug her fingernails into the floor, but still she slid farther from Nick and toward the door.

"Help!"

Hobo leaped onto the creature and sank teeth into its nothingness. For a moment, the Vapor's grasp eased, Chloe's feeling returned, and she ripped her legs free. She stood and flung her body out the window.

Thump.

She quickly rose and whipped around toward the window, glowing brighter blue. Chloe looked at her feet. She had not fallen. Instead, she'd landed on water, and now stood on an ocean or lake so vast she couldn't see its shore. Hobo's bark faded into the distance.

"I'm standing on a lake. I'm not sinking."

Neither was the shack with the blue window from which she'd escaped.

"Okay, none of this is in the movie. Not a lake. Not a floating shack …"

Her legs trembled.

Not me. "Can anybody hear me?" Chloe took an anxious step backward. "Mom? Grandpa?"

Then she heard it.

"Hey! Look at me! Watch me!"

Nick.

She spun and rubbed her eyes. Nick ran. Not a hesitant run, a free run. A confident run. He raced on top of the surface of the water. "I can see. I can see you, Chloe! This is exactly how I wrote it!"

"What are you talking about?"

Nick ran up to her and stopped, his eyes focused and clear. He lifted his finger to her face. "Eyes, nose, mouth, scar. Oh, big scar. I can see it all!" He bounded off.

Chloe reached up and stroked her neck. *Still me.* "Where are we, Nick?"

"Retinya. My screenplay. When my screenplay fell and your film snapped, the two must have spliced together into one story and … oh, who cares? We're here!" He leaped and pumped both fists. "And I'm not blind in Retinya!"

Chloe grabbed his arm. "That's great. That's —
But how do we get home?"

"Home? Who wants to go home? Chloe, I can
see."

"But what about your family and Hobo?"

Nick paused. "I'm not going back through *that*
window." He pointed at the grayish arms still reaching out toward them. "If you want to go, that's your
business. But I'm going on a walk, a long, sighted
walk, that-a-way!" He pointed away from the shack,
and started to skip. "I forgot how beautiful blue was!"

Chloe glanced back at the window.

"Hobo, are you still in there?" She listened, heard
nothing, and cupped her hands. "Hey, Nick, did you
write another go-home window ahead? I left the
ending to you, so I don't know what's there ..."

Nick didn't answer either.

Chloe shook her head. "Oh, Grandpa Salvador,
what do I do?"

Grandpa Salvador loved to dream. While he slept, Grandpa said he sailed through the air, met old friends, and explored the Arctic. "I wake with a smile on my face, dear Chloe. It is a wonderful way to greet a day."

Chloe's dreams rarely brought smiles. She routinely fell off cliffs, suffocated, or received fatal war wounds in dark, desolate lands. This was Chloe's first clue that she may not be dreaming, for she stood in bright light with no sense of dread.

Clumps of white mist rose from the surface of the lake on which she stood and skimmed over her shoes. It was a strange, weighty mist. She bent over and found it smooth and solid to the touch.

What did you dream up, Nick? Wait … what did we dream up?

Chloe stared at the fog. "I changed the lake with Hobo. I know we did. If I remember right, if I step up on top of the fog ..." She gently placed her foot on the mist. The wispy patch skimmed forward. It was waterskiing without touching the water.

"You've got to be kidding!" Chloe smiled, hopped aboard, and away she zoomed. The lake sparkled like glass, and behind her, fish jumped and splashed in her wake.

"I invented this! Well, according to Grandpa, Aldo had the idea first, but I put it on paper!"

Her hair whipped her face and it took effort to keep balanced, yet she found that with many tiny weight shifts, she could remain upright. Inside, a feeling awoke, one dormant since the loss of her horse. Chloe felt free, alive, and her heart wanted the ride to last forever.

Her legs didn't.

A deep ache soon eclipsed the thrill, and she tottered, bent down, then steadied on all fours. Chloe caught her breath and tried to recall all the scenes she had described, all the places she knew in Retinya, but this didn't feel like anyplace from the script. Still her heart quickened, like she was near something familiar, something good.

Finally, her transport slowed, and Chloe straightened. Ahead, she saw a thin, brown shoreline. Nick stood in front of it, standing on his own wispy patch. As Chloe came to a hovering stop feet from land, she stepped out onto the water and marched forward.

"Stop!" Nick grabbed her wrist. "Stop here."

"Why? I'm stuck in your world, so I might as well look around."

"We're not in Retinya yet, but I just found out something about this place." Nick reached into his pocket and took out his house keys. He tossed them onto shore, where they disappeared into the dirt with a splash.

"Nothing is as it seems," he whispered. "That's where we are. Nothing is as it seems."

Chloe stared at Nick. "We can't walk on land? What can we do? I need the rules, at least until I come to something I recognize. There were entire scenes missing when you gave me the script ... this must be one of them. I figured you knew what was supposed to happen. You do, right?"

Nick gnawed his lip. "I don't know any more than you, other than Lake Atmos. That was mine, but these little fog riders, I don't know where they came from—"

"Me!" Chloe smiled. "I put those in."

Nick peered around nervously. "So we're stuck in a gap, sort of like a black hole, and we need to find

Retinya, but we don't know anything or how to get there." He rubbed his face and moaned. "Why didn't I fill in the pages right after the lake?"

Chloe breathed in deeply. "I wouldn't say we don't know *anything*. I sort of stuck a character in this space, you know, for future use. But until we find him, what do people in this world eat? Did you make notes about that? Please tell me there are nachos or burritos in this place. If you knew how hungry —"

"Come over here, Chloe."

To her right, a young man, maybe Q's age, sat in a rowboat and bobbed in the sandy shore. He poled his tiny boat directly in front of Chloe.

"Nob, at your service, lady. It'd be my pleasure to take you to food." He paused and winked. "And a meetin'."

"Don't go." Nick gulped.

Nob frowned and pointed. "Who is this?" He jabbed Nick's chest with his pole. "It can't be the other one." He glanced around and frowned. "If he was, I would have seen Scout. Scout's never late." He squinted at Nick. "Is this boy giving you trouble? Did he follow you?"

"No." Chloe smiled. "I followed him."

"You know this guy?" Every inch of Nick seemed to be frowning.

Chloe felt her cheeks warm. "Yeah, I thought about him once or twice."

Nob's face was young and kind, with long, wild brown hair. His clothes were ripped and tattered, with suspenders holding up trousers shredded at the bottom. He resembled the actor in *Tom Sawyer*, except that Nob's arm muscles rippled.

"That's Nick." Chloe swept back the hair from her face and gave Nob a sideways glance. "You are just going to help me find something to eat."

Nob crossed his pole over his chest. "It's a promise."

"Nick? Stop looking at me like that. It does us no good to die of starvation arguing on a patch of fog."

Nob reached out his hand and helped Chloe into his boat. "Will your friend be joining?"

"No, he will not be joining." Nick crossed his arms. "How do I know where you'll take us?"

The boatman nodded. "You absolutely don't. It takes trust." He smiled at Chloe. "And now, let's see about you, lady."

"Lady." *That's a nickname!* Chloe pointed back to her cloud transport. "When you first called me, how did you know my name?" she asked. "I mean, I know you. I thought you up, right? But you ..."

Nob chuckled and pushed back with his pole.

"Thinkin' you created me now, huh? You must come from a very strange world."

"Wait!" Nick reached out to the boat, breathing hard. "I'm coming. I'm not letting you take her away."

Chloe smiled. "How very knightly of you."

Soon Nob's rowboat whisked through high grass, which parted and rippled as it rushed by.

Nick bent over and whispered, "You wrote him in. What's he like?"

"Like Bert." Chloe grinned.

"Bert and Ernie? *Sesame Street*?"

"No, like Bert the chimney sweep in *Mary Poppins*. He treated Mary like a fine —"

"Lady, hold on. You too, lad. It gets bumpy from here."

Chloe slipped into the bottom of the boat and grabbed her seat. "Then don't you think *you* should sit — whoa!"

The boat pitched and lilted. Nob had reached a hill, but instead of floating around it, he poled straight up its side. They reached the top, tipped over the edge and, like the water ride at Valleyfair, plummeted down. A soaking combination of green grass and brown earth splashed over their heads.

"How many more?" Chloe sputtered.

Nob didn't answer. He powered their way up the

next hill, and the next, each one larger and steeper than the one before. Chloe's stomach lurched; the empty spot now felt only sick.

She closed her eyes and curled up in the boat. Nick thunked down beside her. "Your help is trying to kill us!"

Dirt washed over them, and Chloe fought back sobs. "You were right. We should never have left the lake."

"Not now, lady." Nob's kind, calm voice drifted to her ears. "Wipe your eyes. We're almost there."

She sat up, and immediately the boat jarred into a firm bank that looked no different than the liquid earth.

"See?" Nob leaped out of the boat and spread his arms. "Solid." He helped Chloe onto dry land. "And here I'll be waitin'. Never do I go beyond this point."

Chloe stopped. "Hold on. You're not coming? I came for food. How do I find it?"

"It's not so much that you need to find anything. Just put yourself in a nice place where you can be found."

Totally a Grandpa Salvador sentence.

"Come on, Chloe. We don't need him." Nick jumped out and trudged ahead.

She turned from Nick to Nob. "Nob, do you know where I'm from? This doesn't feel like a dream, but it's not real either. Am I asleep?"

"I don't know where you've come from. I don't know if you're dreaming." Nob lay down in the boat. "I know I was sent to collect the two of you — and I have. And I can't go with you because what you hear is for you alone." He nestled down and closed his eyes. "I'll be waiting, or resting ... or maybe sleeping."

Chloe's stomach growled. "I see that helpfulness was not a trait I wrote into your character!" She rejoined Nick, and together they walked toward a line of trees, feet soon crunching the twigs carpeting a lovely wood. She rubbed moss and stroked bark — the trees felt real and solid and smelled of oak and maple, the same aroma that hung lazily along the banks of the Snake. The scent calmed her.

Mom's got to be panicking right now. She'll freak when I tell her.

And just like that, the wood ended, and Chloe blinked in the warmth and light of a large clearing.

"Anything look familiar?" Nick asked.

Chloe blinked hard. "The trees, where we just were, it felt like home, except — "

"Shh!" hissed Nick. "Listen."

Humming. Chloe heard humming. But this was a man hum, and it struck her ears as odd. Unlike the noises her dad and his workers made — too loud and too wild — this sound was deep and soft, and she stretched her neck to see.

Across the clearing was a garden — a garden Chloe's mom would love, filled with rich, black dirt. The plot spanned at least two acres, and in it, bent over a hoe, was the hummer.

He was an average-sized man, dressed no differently than the migrant workers she'd seen in fields back home. A loose shirt hung on his tan, worked body, and sturdy boots protected his feet. Chloe couldn't see any house nearby, but this property was every bit as beautiful as Finnegan's.

He doesn't seem dangerous.

"You'd be surprised." The man straightened and turned as he waved them closer. "You're hungry. You've had a long day." He nodded toward a small grove of fruit trees near the garden's edge. Oranges, apples, and pears hung large and inviting, and Chloe's throat burned.

"It's yours for the picking."

Chloe didn't need to be told again. She jogged into the grove and ate until sticky juice coated her chin and neck and her insides were content.

"Can you believe how this tastes?" She plucked one last handful of grapes from a wandering vine and stuffed them in her mouth, then turned a slow circle. "Nick?"

Chloe stared back toward the woods. Nick still stood at the edge, rubbing his stomach and staring at the trees.

"Why won't you eat?"

"He is terrified of me," the gardener said quietly.

Chloe walked toward the man slowly. He was reaching for his walking stick. Reaching and grasping and not finding.

He can't see! Chloe tiptoed up to the edge of the dirt and clasped the stick. She raised it and bumped his hand with its free end, and he slowly wrapped fingers around it.

"Nick, he's blind. What are you frightened of?"

"That's just it!" called Nick, his voice shaking. "Blind and useless. That's how I wrote him."

"Wrote who — Wait, Secholit? The one I wasn't supposed to touch? Retinya's hero?"

Chloe looked back to the garden. "I was hoping that you could . . . I see you probably can't, but . . . can you get me home?" Chloe asked.

"Possibly." Secholit trudged between two perfect rows of three-inch holes, stopped, and pulled out a seed from the pouch at his side. He pressed that seed deep into the ground and carefully mounded dirt over the top.

"Now, Chloe, I've left my water bucket. Could you reach it to me?"

She rushed over, grabbed the bucket, and placed the handle in his outstretched hand.

"Thank you." He sprinkled water onto the mound, sat back, and waited.

One minute passed. Five minutes.

Chloe cleared her throat. "Um. Nothing grows that fast." *You wouldn't see it if it did.*

"Quiet now." He raised his finger, placed it over her lips, and faced the lump.

"How did you know where I — ?"

A tiny shoot broke through the ground and opened, revealing a pale green sphere, round and perfect, about the size of a quarter. The man stroked the plant, plucked the bulb, and set it gently into the air, where it hung like an old helium balloon.

Then he blew.

It whisked upward, but it didn't vanish from sight. In fact, it did quite the opposite, growing larger the farther it traveled, until its shadow enveloped the entire glade.

"What is it?" Chloe stared.

"It's a world," he said quietly. He stood and faced the greenish mammoth. "Now go, find your place."

As if its tether broke, the planet shot into the distance, shrinking until it disappeared entirely.

Chloe swallowed hard. "This garden's not in my astronomy textbook. You, uh, really grow worlds?"

"At times." He sat down in the dirt. "But now I am interested solely in you and your friend."

She nodded, but said nothing.

"You're a long way from home," he said. "From your dad and your mom, your brothers and your grandpa."

Grandpa Salvador.

His kind face entered her mind, and Chloe broke down. "I miss him most of all. I want to be home! I know we kind of made you up — I mean, made this world up — but I wasn't ever planning on coming here."

Secholit smiled. "Nick didn't invent me, and I understand that coming here was not a part of your plan. Hiding in a projection booth is much more comfortable."

"How do you know about — "

He gradually pressed his toe into the soil. "From this plot of land, you can see far. Even without eyes. It was for this world that you were called. There's much here that, I believe, you could make right."

Chloe quieted and peeked into Secholit's face. "But the place is beautiful. If you could see the trees, the land. Everything's already right."

"This world stretches far beyond this glade, Chloe. Don't believe your task is simply to eat fruit."

"What's he saying, Chloe? Whatever it is, ignore it. He's not the strongest one in Retinya. We can get help somewhere else. We don't have to listen to a blind man. We can see!"

Chloe thought a moment. "Actually, that makes sense. Nick's right. My task is *not* to stay, but get home." She slumped. "Listen, you seem really nice. But you just made a world. Whatever needs doing, I'm sure you can handle it. If you can start me on my way, we'll both be happy."

Secholit rose slowly, leaned hard on his walking stick, and strode to the far side of the garden. There he felt around for his shovel, found it, and dug a deep hole. He winced himself straight and leaned on the handle, face to the sky. Chloe followed his empty gaze.

A tiny black speck whizzed across the clear blue. It grew, took shape, until it resembled a raven or crow, but soon it was too large for that. It was a man. A man's dark shadow screaming nearer.

"Down," Secholit called, and the shadow plunged

into the hole. Dirt exploded on impact and hung in the air. Chloe could barely make out the gardener's shape as he buried the thing.

"What was that?" Chloe asked.

"I'm not sure," he called, and set down the shovel. "So you won't help us."

"I didn't say that. I'm just suffering from a tremendous lack of information. That and I think that you could do whatever it is better than I."

He walked back toward her. "I could. But if you do it, it won't be undone. Besides, who would do my sowing?"

Chloe winced. "You mean the world-making thingy and the shadow planting deal? Yeah. That might be beyond me." She paced. "For the sake of argument, and I'm not arguing or anything, what's the job?"

Secholit stopped an arm's length away. He reached up and touched the scar on Chloe's chin. She wanted to pull away, but found she couldn't move until he lowered his hand.

"Help this world remember. Help Retinya remember."

He spun and walked back into his garden, reached into his pocket, and removed a seed.

"That's it?" Chloe raised both hands. "That's all I

get? Help? Help *how*? And where exactly is Retinya? And maybe tell me what you've forgotten. Details are really helpful 'cause I only wrote a part of the script."

Secholit mounded dirt and sat down to wait. "For now, that's enough. And Chloe, for now that message is just for you and Nick."

"What message? The remembering thing? You haven't told me — "

"You will need Nick, and you will need help. So I'm sending my ferryman, Nob, to start you on your way. He won't take kindly to the idea, but he will take you down."

"Down? You realize I haven't agreed yet, right?" She double fisted her hair and pulled. "Ah! Is this really that important?"

"You're here." He pointed at the woods. "Which makes me believe it is. Chloe, I gave you a glimpse of this world before you came. You wrote down what was in your mind. You drew what you saw. This was a gift. In a way, you've been here for some time already. Remember what you've seen; remember what you know." He pointed toward the grove. "Now, go back the way you came, and remember, Chloe Lundeen, you are very beautiful."

Fine. She stomped away from the garden, rubbing her scar and rolling her eyes.

Wait. Very beautiful?

Her jaw tightened, and then sprung loose. "You have no idea what I look like. You're a blind liar, trying to make the ugly girl feel better so she does you a favor. And you've got it backward. How could you give us anything? We made you!" Chloe spun back toward the garden. "So maybe keep your mouth … shut."

The man was gone. His tools were gone. And in the middle of the garden, his walking stick poked out of the ground.

She rubbed her forehead. "Calm down, Chloe. If this is a dream, just go with it. If it's not … Nick?" She couldn't see him anywhere. She suddenly felt very weak, and very alone.

I didn't even thank the guy for the fruit.

CHLOE FOUND NICK SITTING on the ground near a snoring Nob. She bumped Nick with her foot. "Why do you keep leaving me?"

"He was supposed to be strong. In control. Secholit was supposed to be the coolest blind guy ever. But there's nothing cool about being blind." Nick shook his head. "Did you see him grope around that garden? What a loser."

"When you were blind, you were never a loser. Remember that." Nick refused to meet her eye. "Oh!" Chloe exhaled. "He gave us a task. Both of us. We need to help Retinya remember. That's what he said. Did you write anything about that?"

"No." Nick rolled his eyes, stood, and looked down at Nob. "Should we wake our transportation?"

Chloe shook Nob's shoulder. He smiled, muttered, and rolled over.

"Nob!"

He slowly opened his eyes, and then yawned and stretched. "Did you have a good visit?"

"A good visit," Chloe repeated. "Couldn't have been better. We ate fruit, watched a world hatch, saw a shadow buried ... You know, the typical. You could have filled me in a bit more before you sent us off to meet that guy."

"I told you what you needed."

"Well, you'll have plenty more chances to do that. You're supposed to take us down, whatever that means."

His face whitened. "Secholit said that?"

"Yeah." Chloe glanced toward the woods. "The blind guy in the garden."

Nob scratched his head. "I'm not the right one for that. I really ought to stay up here. A ferryman. That's my job, that's what I'm good at. I, uh ..."

"He said you'd say that too." Chloe's shoulders slumped. "Listen, I need your help. I don't want to go any more than you do, but Nick and I need to get home, and there's some job he thinks we should do first and ... Oh, it's all miserable."

Nob stepped out of the boat and began to pace. "Do you know what's below?"

Chloe pointed to her face. "Do I look like I know what's below?"

Nob rubbed his chin, hard. "You're sure he said me? By name?"

Chloe stepped toward Nob and pressed her finger into his chest, and then gestured toward the garden. "I don't know many Nobs. Why not just go ask him if you don't believe me?"

"The thing is, I haven't spoken to him in years. Certainly never asked him anything. I don't like to get too close, if you know my meaning."

"Yeah," Nick said. "I do."

"No!" Chloe said, "I don't. You sent me to see — Forget it. Forget it!" Chloe held up her hand. "You're taking us down."

"Oh, lady. This is the worst of days."

Chloe sat quietly as they poled back toward the lake, while Nick cleaned his fingernail with a piece of wood he'd found inside the boat. The entire time Nob muttered and stammered, "Bad choice. Really bad choice." Finally, the ferry struck the water.

Nob rocked back and forth, thumbed his suspenders. "I never thought I'd see this day." His gaze fell and for a moment, he teetered.

"What's wrong?" Nick kept working that fingernail.

Nob forced a smile and shook his head. "I haven't been below for years. It's easier not having to be near the man now that he's changed."

"What man?" Chloe waited and shrugged. "Doesn't sound like you've seen much of anybody."

Nob straightened and looked across the lake. "I'm not going to be good at this. Flit!"

From below the surface of the water exploded a gigantic eagle, at least it looked like one from beneath — though the head, wings, and top appeared more dragon than bird. Its back was gray and scarred, its wings wrinkled and worn, but underneath feathers ruffled thick and white and inviting. Even though the creature was enormous, Chloe longed to press her hand into the down.

The dragonbird spread its leathery wings and landed softly.

"What news, Flit?"

"News," it croaked. "You don't hear this news and feel joy. All is confusion. Be glad you live above — "

"Secholit sends me down," Nob interrupted. "We need transport."

Flit's head twitched and cocked. "Down? What did you do, Nob? And of all the times — the cursed Pilgrimage begins."

Nob shook his head, and Flit's great eyes danced from Nick to Chloe. "Three passengers. We will be breaking through, so it will involve two trips."

"I'll go first." Nick stepped forward. "Anything to get away from this nothing place. Besides, once I reach Retinya, I'll be fine. I'd like a little time there alone." He glanced over his shoulder. "Chloe, I'll wait for you."

"You're not leaving me again." Chloe walked toward Nick.

"And you are not leaving my sight, lady." Nob caught up quickly.

Flit closed his eyelids. "Humans." He reached out with one talon and pulled Nick into his under feathers. "What do you seek alone that you cannot find with a guide?"

"None of your business, you freaky lizard. Can we go?"

Chloe turned to Nob and whispered, "Don't let Nick go by himself. Something's happening to him. He's always been harsh, but he's changing, and I don't quite understand how, but I feel it and—"

Crack!

Chloe spun. "Where are they?" She ran onto the lake and circled around. "Nob!"

"They've gone. Lady, I will say this one time, and

then hold my tongue as he is your friend. There is an evil about Nick."

"Evil? Mean, maybe. Cruel, I'll give you that one. Arrogant, proud, self-absorbed — but not evil."

"Did he go toward Secholit when called?"

"No." Chloe's voice lowered. "He hid in the woods. But I get that. I mean, I hide sometimes too."

"And where do you think he goes now?" Nob's voice was monotone. "What, or who, does he look for?"

"No idea. He knows a lot about Retinya, much more than I do."

"He will go somewhere familiar, to something he knows." Nob stared at Chloe. "Let me ask you. Is he used to darkness?"

"Well, yeah. He lived in it back home."

"Darkness isn't confined to your world, lady."

Flit screeched from behind and Chloe leaped. "I've not met a more disagreeable human."

Chloe ran forward and Flit rose to full height. He was as big as her barn. "Where did you leave him?" Flit glanced at Nob. Chloe did too. Nob's face tightened.

"What?" Chloe stomped toward her guide. "What aren't you telling me?"

"In time, lady." Nob turned to Flit. "I suppose we're ready."

Flit's wings churned the air, and Chloe fought to stand against the wind. Slowly, he rose, lifted each traveler with his talons, and pulled them into his feathery underside.

"Prepare," he thundered. Higher and higher he circled until the lake was no more than a patch of blue. Flit dipped a wing, and for a moment they were weightless. Then he turned downward. Faster, faster, he hurtled toward the water, the solid water. Chloe braced herself, burying her head into Flit's soft underbelly.

Crack. They burst through the lake and thundered downward. Chloe stretched her neck around and looked up.

Sky. She really had been walking on the sky. Aldo's moving transport billowed against a field of blue. Below them was the ground, and it looked not unlike it does from inside an airplane, except it approached with frightening speed.

"Nob!"

The wind swallowed Chloe's scream, and they veered and plummeted toward a forest so thick she could not see to its floor. They did not slow; in fact, if anything Flit gained speed. She braced again, but Flit swooped and Chloe shrieked, her feet dangling inches from the canopy. Ahead, the forest stretched unbroken to the horizon.

Flit flashed his wings and came to an abrupt stop, hovering over the trees.

"Good-bye, friends." His talons opened and Chloe dropped into the upper leaves.

Normally, Chloe's tree climbing adventures were scratchy experiences. But this was altogether different. Her landing was soft, much like the jump into a pile of fall leaves. She sank deep into the tree, all light vanishing as branches filled in above her.

In the black nothingness, fingers rounded her waist. "Nob? What are you — Oh!"

Chloe grasped at the hand and recoiled; it was rough like bark.

"Are you even here, Nob?"

"Lady!" Nob's voice sounded distant.

"Let me go!" Chloe beat on the wooden fist, which hoisted her forward. She yelled and struck it again, loosening the grip. She was free, but only for a moment. Another hand clasped around her.

The trees! I've been handed off like a human baton.

She zipped through the forest, passed from one tree to another.

Then, light.

A dull beacon shone far ahead. But in pitch darkness, even a dull glow has effect. It grew stronger, but not sharper. The soft, blue beam enveloped her, and she could see the hands that held her.

Sure enough, strong, knotty fingers held her from the ends of moveable branches. And the light ahead revealed a village of shadow. Silhouetted against a deep, leafy background perched the most impressive tree houses she'd ever seen. Set at different heights, the dwellings ranged from simple, square constructions to multilevel masterpieces. The blue light shone out every window, and in that glow Chloe caught sight of the inhabitants.

They swung on vines like howler monkeys at the zoo. Their stocky bodies zipped silently from house to house and branch to branch, barely avoiding collision in the chaotic dance. Children clapped as they whisked by each other. Others swung in pairs and trios.

Incredible.

"Nob!" Chloe hissed.

"Elves." Nob leaned into her shoulder. "Great. My good luck continues."

Chloe's jaw fell open. "Elves? I love this part. They're the kindest, most trusting, most generous creatures in this whole world, and I should know."

"Uh. Perhaps you should let me do the speakin', lady. They hear what lies beneath your words."

"What does that mean?"

"It means we hear more than you say." An elf swung onto the branch in front of her. "And you say much more than you know."

Chloe rubbed her eyes and stared. They didn't look like any elves she'd seen in the movies. They weren't pudgy, Santa types, nor tall and fair, dressed in green or white with a bow at the back and a quiver at the side.

These elves were all eyes. Big, searching eyes that had lived too long blanketed by darkness.

"You're supposed to be tall. You're supposed to live in an elf kingdom on the forest floor." Chloe frowned.

"You describe what we were and what was. But you're a thousand years too late to see any such sight." The elf raised a stone to Chloe's face. It glowed pale and blue, and in that light she felt his searching gaze come to rest on her scar.

"Lost One." He reached toward Chloe's chin and she jerked away. "What a shame."

"No. She's never been to the pool." Nob laid a hand on the elf's shoulder. "She's new to this place." To Chloe he murmured, "And she is supposed to stay quiet."

The elf shifted the stone to Chloe's guide,

chuckled, and pulled away. "Seems to be a familiar story these days. Children just popping into the world." He squinted. "Well, if it isn't Brave Nob! Does Scout know you're here?"

Nob remained silent.

"It has been some time. Are there not more to ferry above ... or did you return for personal reasons?"

Nob swallowed hard. "Hael, you mentioned another child. Did it happen to be a boy—"

"His name's Nick! He came right before we did." Chloe slapped her hand over her mouth.

The elf gazed into her with those eyes. "Why do you look for a boy you hate?"

"I don't ... I mean, I don't think I hate—"

It was Nob's turn to cover Chloe's mouth. "We just want safe passage out of the forest, and any word you have of the boy. He can't be too far in front of us." He rolled his eyes, and his jaws tightened. "Apparently he's important," he muttered. "Fool Flit. Why he dropped us here ..."

"Much has changed since you've last walked in the lower world. But come. I've now heard what you want. Let's find out what you need." Hael rapped three times on the tree that held Chloe fast. "Ease, friend." The wooden hand released, and she and Nob scrambled after the elf.

Chloe always thought herself an excellent climber. But in the hazy blue light, she lost her balance several times, staying aloft due only to Nob's quick hands. With him, she felt safe. She could not say this about the elf.

Hael led them at a horrific pace. Up, down, around, more squirrel than upright creature. Several bumps and bruises later, Chloe scampered after Hael into a full-sized cottage, situated among the gnarly oaks.

"Stay." Hael's eyes twinkled in the blue light.

"For how long?" Chloe stomped the sturdy floor. "I don't know where I am and Nick probably doesn't either, and I just want to do what I have to do and find Nick and get home to Mom and Grandpa Salvador and ..."

A voice boomed from behind. "And who?"

CHAPTER

12

CHLOE WHIPPED AROUND. There on the ground sat an elf, legs crossed, wearing the largest hat Chloe'd seen. She longed to touch that hat — brown and kinked and pointed — with a brim so wide it hid his entire face. The elf sat so still, blended in so well, he looked like part of the wall in his long coat of knotty brown. Chloe bent way over and frowned. No pointed ears.

"Leave us, Hael," the seated elf said quietly. He turned to Chloe. "Mom and Salvador, yes. But there is someone else at the end of that sentence, someone you want to see most of all."

Chloe said nothing and peeked at Nob, who groaned and threw up his arms.

"So this is not speaking?"

She turned back to the elf. "There's nobody else I miss."

"Your scar is long. Are you certain you haven't simply forgotten?"

Nob stepped in front of her. "As I told your watchman, she is new to this world."

"And yet both of you search for the same thing."

"A young boy, yes." Nob stepped forward.

"No." The elf rose and grasped his hands behind his back. "Fathers."

Being far from Crazy Ray is the only good thing about being here.

"But enough for now. I apologize for Hael's rough treatment. As our outermost watch, he sees few wanderers. The excitement of three is a bit much."

Chloe shook thoughts of Dad from her mind and started to speak, then squeezed tight her lips.

The elf smiled. "Yes, the trees caught the boy, but did not receive him in. He is not here now. I doubt you will see him again." He strode toward the door and grasped one of the vines that hung outside the opening. "I'm not certain if he truly was a boy. Hael said he wore darkness about him." The chieftain cleared his throat. "But now allow me to be your host. It's been many years since my last interested visitor, and this chief longs to show you Mystal in its fullness."

Nob followed him to the doorway, and Chloe took a slow step. Nob raised his eyebrows. "We're about to see a place only imagined around campfires."

Chloe grasped a vine. "But that elf knew your name. You haven't been here?"

"Names are worn like clothing," interrupted the chief. "They aren't hidden." He paused and winked at her. "But they are occasionally forgotten."

I remember just fine, thank you.

"Can we please go?" Chloe asked.

The chief gestured into the emptiness outside the doorway. "Yes. The question is, can you swing?"

Chloe spent the next hour swinging from tree to tree, house to house, storehouse to meeting hall. Elves dodged and ducked in front of her — it took a while to learn unmarked aerial paths. But after a few close calls, she mastered the art of midair vine changing, as well as the whistle that warned others of an approach. Her hair flew in the breeze, and it felt glorious.

"Your kingdom, the invisible one deep in the forest along the Wandering Road, where is it?" Chloe called. "I know it's here. It has to be."

The chief swung up beside Chloe. "How do you know of that place?" He whistled, and two young elves parted before them. "It is no more. The road you speak of is now just a remnant. Few elves remember." The chief removed his hat and scratched his scraggly hair. "Perhaps tonight all our questions will be answered. I think you will meet Scout. You aren't the only one eager to find the boy. We'll hear your words in the Cleft and learn what we can from them. But for now, follow me."

They swung into an empty room, and the chief inspected it thoroughly. "Your room for the afternoon, Chloe."

"Is it really afternoon? It feels like midnight."

The chief smiled, reached into his pocket, and pulled out a blue stone. "Mountain stone follows the rhythm of the outside. During the day, the blue burns bright. When it is all but gone, it is eve, and I will come for you."

Chloe rolled the stone over in her hand. "Can I keep it?"

A grin worked the edge of the chieftain's mouth. "If you survive tonight's meeting, yes. Just know that outside the forest, these stones take on certain ... other qualities."

"If I survive?" Chloe asked.

The chief turned to Nob. "Now come. Tell me how you came to Retinya once again."

Nob nodded and glanced over his shoulder.

"You're safe now, Chloe. Get rest. Tonight will be a night you'll need to remember."

After fighting to put her mind to ease, Chloe woke to singing. Not light, fair singing like that in the movie *Elvenking*. This was deep and sorrowful. She rose and wandered to the window. Her blue stone glowed dimly.

Nob swung into the doorway. "They want us."

"Where have you been this entire time?" she asked. "I thought you were supposed to stay with me."

"I never claimed to be a good guide. For that you'd want another."

Nob stepped backward and swung out into the darkness.

Stuck in an alternate world with an unreliable guide. Perfect.

Chloe clutched a vine and followed. Together they crossed through the village, swooping toward the song. They passed the last dwelling, and as the blue light faded behind them, Chloe saw less and less until …

Her vine struck something firm above, and she flung forward. The temperature cooled dramatically, and her hands lost their firm grip in the dank air. Down she slid, toward the song rising up from below. Blanketed by cold, Chloe released her hold completely and landed on a slab of rock. Slowly, she straightened, for the first time in a day on solid ground.

Chloe turned a slow circle. In place of trees, dimly glowing stones surrounded her. Hundreds, maybe thousands of elves sat on every rocky outcropping. She had clearly swung into a massive mountain cave. Outside its mouth, she saw the forest of vines and branches.

"Welcome to the Cleft, Nob, Chloe. It was here that we fought the Great Battle, here that we safe-guard the only source of mountain stone." The sing-ing stopped at the sound of the chief's voice. "Young lady, you pose a dilemma. A problem."

"What did I do wrong?"

"You came."

Elves murmured in agreement.

"I did not — Well, I didn't *mean* to come. I was called, or sent, or told, sort of." Chloe buried her face in her hands. "And I couldn't leave Nick. I need to find him. This is so confusing."

The chief approached. "Yes, Nob has told me." He turned, scaled the cave wall, and reclined in a chair, an azure throne carved entirely of mountain stone and covered with elf etchings. The chieftain's body shone.

"If we knew that you were sent by Secholit, we would certainly lend you aid. Unfortunately for you, that Nob fled Secholit in his hour of need is well known. I find it highly doubtful that Secholit would trust him to guide anyone of importance … would trust him to guide anyone at all."

"Whoa. Stop right there." Chloe raised her hand and turned to Nob. "You left Secholit? Nick wrote up a battle scene, and I put you in there. You were the hero."

Nob lowered his gaze. "I've not been heroic for some time."

"How do we know she's not a Senseri?" a voice from the darkness whispered, and the question repeated, gained strength.

"Look at the scar. She's a Lost One, for sure. Nobody else could have found us."

Nob yelled, "Would Flit bring a Senseri to this place?"

"He brought the boy." Hael stepped forward, gesturing to the entire assembly. "The boy acted every bit the Senseri."

Nob stepped forward. "Flit did not know what the boy was."

"Who knows if it was Flit?" Hael spoke to the chief. "None on the outer watch saw a dragon. You know that Flit's siblings have turned. It's just a matter of time until he also —"

The chief held up his hand, and the great cave fell silent. "Let her own words affirm or condemn. Chloe, tell me who you are."

Chloe gazed over at Nob, who nodded. "You know my name." She raised both hands. "I'm Chloe Lundeen from Melmanie, Minnesota. I don't know how I got here. I was in Aldo's Movie Palace, which is the movie house my great-grandfather built. I was showing a film called *The Vapor* — terrible acting, by the way — and then suddenly I was in *The Vapor*, with Nick, and then the blue window appeared and —"

"Stop." The chief held up a finger.

The air around Chloe was heavy with silence. Nobody breathed.

"A blue window," the chief repeated.

"Yeah. Blue. Nick claims he wrote that, but Grandpa was into blue before we left and I was the one who — Oh, it doesn't matter. We climbed through it and we were on a lake, actually a sky, and then we met Nob."

The chief stood. "So there is a window above. Tell me, does it look like this?" He looked out into the gathering. "Hael!"

Hael scampered up beside the chief. "With all respect, she's admitted to seeing Vaepor, to being in the palace. It already controls one window. If It were to find the second, what would stop It from seeing freely throughout Retinya and destroying—"

"Hael." The chief laid a hand on Hael's head. "You have heard for yourself. There is nothing but truth behind her words." He gestured upward. "Lift the veil."

Hael hung his head, reached forward, grabbed a gray, rocky outcrop and twisted. The rock face spun like a revolving door, and next to the glowing throne appeared a window, blue and perfect.

"That's it!" she pointed.

"Come up, Chloe." The chief gestured. "Nob, you as well."

Together, they climbed up the rough wall and leaned on the sill. "I can't see through." Chloe turned toward the chief. "I just see me."

"Keep looking."

Chloe's face faded, and in her place appeared Grandpa Salvador, stepping out of his trailer home for his morning walk.

"Grandpa. I'm right here! Oh, I'm right here! Can I go to him now?" she begged. "Please, let me go through."

"Through this window, you can only see. I have heard of others, ones through which you can step. I knew It kept one in the palace. Now I know the other is in a much safer place."

For the first time during the gathering, the elf chieftain smiled.

Chloe stroked the glass and Salvador disappeared, replaced by Dad in tears, his head bowed, sitting in the hay. Chloe dropped her gaze.

"Your father," said the chief. "You choose not to look at him."

Inside, she felt a burning. "He chooses not to look at me!" She pointed at her face. "Do you think I did this to myself? Believe me, I remember every instant, every insult, every ..." Chloe swallowed hard and peeked over her shoulder at the hundreds of surprised faces.

"It's hard, is all," she said quietly and turned her back toward the window. "I don't need to see him. If that is all this window does, it's worthless. Go ahead, Nob."

"You're sure." He moved over, breathed deeply, and stared.

Chloe peeked over his shoulder. As Dad and the farm disappeared, a dull ache sprung to life inside her and her throat thickened.

Strange. I never missed Dad before.

A coastal town appeared in the window, the light from two moons reflecting off the water. A lone man whistled and walked the dark wharf.

"Who is he?" Chloe asked.

Nob said nothing. He didn't need to. The resemblance was clear and she stepped up to watch Nob's father.

The man froze, and his mouth stilled. He threw a cape over his head with a flourish, and when he emerged he was a little boy.

"No." Nob shook. "When I left, he was not that far gone."

"Where is Scout?" Hael cried. When he received no reply, he raised his arms. "Nob's the blood offspring of a Senseri, come to destroy!" Hael looked over the assembly with wild eyes. "And he's in the Cleft?"

The mass of elves pressed nearer, but the chief raised his hand. "I want to see."

The boy sat down in the road. Approaching from the other direction was a little girl with bread in her hands. The boy spoke. The girl dropped the loaf and fled. Slowly, the lad rose and, with a smile, disappeared behind his cape.

Nob's father emerged, scooped up the bread, and went whistling on his way.

The mirror went black.

Nob stared straight ahead. "He's been in the pool more times than I can count, this is no secret, but I never thought he'd become …"

"Will someone tell me what's going on?" Chloe climbed down off the ledge.

"What more evidence do you need, Chieftain?" an old elf called. "Isn't it clear who they are?"

The chief stared down at Chloe. "It will be. Yes, Chloe, I will tell you what is going on. And I think after my story, your reaction will bring all things to light." He motioned toward Nob. "Remove him, and find Scout."

Nob shook his head and put up no fight. "My dad. He was a good man. He really was a good man." Ten elves quickly led him out of the cave.

"Retinya was not always like this." The elf chieftain leaned back on his throne. "We elves did not always cower in the forest. The old among us remember. The invisible city, yes, it was glorious, providing shelter to all in need along the Wandering Road and protecting Retinya from —"

"The Calainians," Chloe interrupted.

"Yes." He frowned. "From the Calainians. There was a time before, before these trees stood, when the land was beautiful and Blind Secholit lived among us.

"I was a scalawag in those younger days, and more than once my father and I set out for the palace in the east. And not just my father. All Retinyans found justice there. More than justice, peace."

Groups of elves murmured.

"Few here remember Wedion, one of the ancient elves. I, and my friends, mocked his age, his ... speed. My father discovered this and took me to the palace, where I told Blind Secholit of my guilt. I waited for my punishment. But Blind Secholit reached forward, lifted a shadow of shame from me, and tossed it into the pool."

"You lost me." Chloe interrupted. "Why?"

"Because Secholit's pool was not for swimming. His pool was for forgetting. Any wrong tossed into the pool vanished from Retinya's memory forever. In this way, he prevented our anger and our bitterness from destroying us.

"But a boat appeared on the horizon of the Eastern Sea, from beyond the Lost Islands. The sailors, short on food but long on treachery, landed at Port's End and made their way down to the palace, where they mocked Blind Secholit. They dived into his pool and emerged, free from their worst memories. Secholit warned them that entering the pool led to death. And in a way they did die — through frequent trips into the pool, they forgot who they were. These men became It's first Senseri."

"And who is It?" Chloe asked.

"Vaepor."

Chloe gasped.

"You know It."

"Maybe. I mean, the name is really close to … Like I told you, I saw the movie in my world, but it was Nick who wrote that into the screenplay. He called it the Darkness."

"An appropriate name," the chief continued. "Word spread that you could forget pain without enduring the humility of speaking with Blind Secholit, and foolish Retinyans abandoned the difficult and snuck into the pool. Finally, Secholit gave men their desire. He left his palace and his pool and wandered the land. Now he's far away."

Chloe bit her lip. "Then who's in charge of the pool?"

"Vaepor. It blew in from the sea, bringing with It illusions from distant lands. These he layered upon Retinya so thickly that we no longer recognized our own country. Mountains seemed to vanish. Rivers suddenly appeared. But his most potent trickery had nothing to do with topography."

The Cleft felt cooler, and Chloe felt another pang inside. "I don't know if I want to hear anymore — "

"You must!" The chief lowered his voice. "Once a year, on what's called the Day of Reckoning, Vaepor calls all the people of Retinya to a pilgrimage. He invites — forces — them to the palace, and to the pool where they will forget all they hold dear."

Chloe raised her hand. "Lost you again. I mean, that is not how we wrote — What good does that do?"

The chief frowned. "A man who can't remember will follow anyone, will believe anything. If it wasn't for Vaepor's frightening form, It would long ago have seduced all men."

"So whoever swims in that pool forgets everything? Have you gone in too?"

"No. This is why we are here. There are a few men who resist, mostly in the arid regions of the Safelands and in Shadowton, and I've heard that other creatures live in secret. But Old Retinya is no more, and when the old among us die, so will the taste of freedom." He breathed deeply. "In three days' time, all known men begin the march on the Path of Pilgrimage. It ends at the pool, where all recent memories will be stolen — ripped from their minds, and I believe held prisoner in the palace. There is no way to know who has forgotten, who is lost, except the mark." He pointed at Chloe's face. "When a pilgrim dips in the pool, a facial mark appears. After years of forgetting, scars form."

Scarface.

"So you thought I was in the pool," Chloe whispered. "I admit it. There is a name I want to forget.

When I swim in the Snake, for those minutes I do feel free of it ..."

The chief leaped off the throne and landed directly in front of Chloe. He raised his blue stone and peered at her. "Have you been in the pool?"

"No, I've never been anywhere near it! I don't know anything about what you just said."

His lips tightened. "Your words lie."

"She does." An elf grabbed her arm.

"I feel it too!" said another.

"She's seen our window. She can't be allowed to live."

The cave exploded with sounds of deep singing as more strong hands wrapped around her arms and legs.

"No!" Chloe shrieked. "I don't know anything. I've never even seen your pool or the palace or — Wait! I do know something!"

The song died. "I know about Blind Secholit. I think I saw him planting. Right before he sent me. And he sows seed, right?"

Elves drew back and Chloe fell to the ground.

"Think about what you say." The chief reached down and helped her up.

"Well, you won't believe this, but I saw him planting worlds. He was growing worlds right out of the dirt. And he was burying stuff. I saw him bury a shadow. That's the guy, right?"

Again, all was silent.

The chief's eyes widened. "What name would you use for him?"

"Nick and Nob told me his name was Secho-lit. He didn't name himself. I mean, there wasn't enough land to call him a farmer. Mom would call it too big for a garden. In Minnesota, we'd call him a sower."

The chief folded his arms. "A sower. That's what stories say. Every elf in this Cleft knows this. Tell me about the shadow. What grew from that?"

"Uh, nothing. He just buried it. He said he didn't even know what it was." Chloe thought for a moment. "Is he really blind?"

"At times." The chief smiled and turned to the elves. "Perhaps we are quick to rush to judgment. That's Blind Secholit. Can any here deny it?" The chief turned to Chloe. "If he sent you"—he turned and stared at Hael—"then you, Chloe, will have *every* elves' assistance."

Hael squeezed his forehead between thumb and forefinger, and stiffly bowed.

Chloe cleared her throat. "Well, I need Nob, and I need to find Nick. And there's something else the guy told me to do that I don't think I'm supposed to talk about."

The chief nodded. "Then that last task will remain yours. But regarding the boy, perhaps we can set you on course. Everyone, to the trees, and with speed. We make for the Remnant Road —" He paused. "And has anybody seen that blasted Scout?"

• • •

Chloe, Nob, and a small detachment of elves set out at once. They swung for hours, and the hours turned to days, if Chloe's mountain stone glowed true. They rarely stopped, and then only long enough for short naps and to grab a fistful of lingonberries. Nob took extra attention to Chloe's hands, raw and bleeding from the vines, bandaging them as best he could. She didn't complain — the elves' faces held a strange urgency, and she was hushed each time she spoke.

Finally, they stopped. Strong, oaken hands grasped them and Hael pointed down.

"We are above it. The Remnant Road. Before It covered the land with deception, when these trees where saplings, this road stretched into the heart of what is now the Unknown Forest. Now it is overgrown, never used. We have no reason to walk it."

The chieftain interrupted. "This road stretches from the forest in the west to the Eastern Sea and will lead you to the palace, if that's where you wish to go. Although I wish on you another destination." He glanced down, kicked at a branch with his toe. "Retinya is a more beautiful place with you in it."

Chloe opened her mouth, but no sounds came out.

"I hope you will find your friend as well," the chief added. "The trees placed him and his mouth in a boat and sent him down the Green River. It will intersect with this road in short order."

"We get to walk?" Chloe's arms ached, and she slid partway down her vine.

"The ground is evil," called the chieftain. "The land will warn It of your presence. But there are paths that have not sworn allegiance. Use your stone to light the way."

Chloe dug her small mountain stone from her pocket, and two towering oaks lowered her and Nob halfway to the ground. "How will we know where to step?"

"Follow Scout," Hael called. "He knows."

"I don't know a Scout. I haven't met a Scout." She glanced over her shoulder. "I've never seen a ... Scout?"

A new figure hung, silently silhouetted against the forest deep. Chloe lifted the glowing stone and illuminated his face.

The young man did not squint. From the neck up, Scout looked regal, with a proud, noble air. He clearly did not live in the forest — his skin was tanned and weathered, as if he'd walked a thousand miles beneath a burning sun. But from the neck down, all royal appearances vanished. He dressed in a loose shirt, torn and dirty, with trousers that hung from four leather straps that crisscrossed his chest.

"You were never in the script," Chloe said.

"You'd be surprised where I've been." Scout hinted a smile. He then turned and frowned at Nob.

"What's going on?" Chloe asked. "You know each other?"

Scout bowed as well as a young man can while hanging on a vine. "I'm pleased to meet you. I will get you to the city of Medahon, this I promise, though I have no idea why you'd want to go. After that, our paths will likely separate. I have business of my own." He leaned closer. "I only ask that you walk in my steps. Do not stray. Do not step to the left or right. As the chieftain said, the ground is evil — well, most of it."

"Medahon? I love that city! Do you want to hear who designed it?"

Scout whisked down his vine. Chloe sighed and slid the rest of the way to the forest floor, where leaves and branches crackled beneath her feet.

She kicked at the brambles. "This is a road? Nob, what do you think?"

"I can't go," Nob whispered from above.

Chloe stared up. "What? Secholit ordered you. He told you to help me. He — "

"And I have. I — This part is beyond my ability. It wasn't what I was asked to do, not really. I was asked to take you down — "

"And help me!"

Nob gazed at the ground, his words coming quietly. "You don't know what lies ahead, but I do. I lived here."

"That's not true. I know this city and its beautiful walls and wild staircases and ... I know where we are. I drew the map! I sketched you from nothing! In *Mary Poppins* Bert could do anything. You're just like him. You can do this."

"Chloe?" Scout's hard stare never left Nob, and he gestured with his hand.

"Please, Nob," she mouthed.

Nob took a deep breath. "Good-bye, lady." He tapped the tree and his vine shot upward.

Good-bye back. She buried her face in her hands. *What should I do?*

"Stay in the forest if you wish." Scout hobbled around and limped away.

Wonderful. Now I have a limping guide.

"Wait for me!"

They weaved forward through the trees, although forward is not quite the correct word. They walked sideways, backward — every direction. But after some hours Chloe noticed the forest changing. There was firmness beneath her feet. Fewer branches crackled, and winks of light pierced the canopy and lit up the forest floor.

The tree line stopped abruptly and they stood, blinking in daylight. Scout glanced over his shoulder and stretched out his arms. "Welcome to Retinya."

It was beautiful. Lakes dotted rolling hills. It looked like Minnesota, but with more valleys.

"It doesn't look right. It feels like Retinya — don't get me wrong — and it is really pretty — "

"Yes." Scout forced a smile. "On the outside." He turned and grabbed Chloe's shoulders. "If we meet anybody on the way, not one word."

"I'm not very good at that."

"Walk beside me. Most of the ground beneath us is on our side."

Chloe soon had passed him. She glanced back at Scout, whose gaze never left the path. In the light, his limp was far more pronounced.

"Your leg ..."

Scout caught up and they moved on the wide road together. Beneath them, dirt changed to gravel and then to fitted rock. "You aren't used to walking so slowly."

"Actually, I am." The thought of morning walks with Grandpa made her smile. She closed her eyes. She could see the tall grass, the cows in the distance.

Take my arm, Chloe. We will make a good show.

"You will want to hide that."

Chloe opened her eyes and stared at the stone in her hand, burning blue. She jammed it in her pocket, but the light fought its way out.

"Wait here. On the road." Scout kept his eyes on her pocket. "I'll gather some lunch."

Chloe watched Scout hobble off the cobblestones, work his way up a hill, and disappear. She sighed and plunked down on the lonely road. She traced her finger in the sand that filled the spaces between the paving stones.

"Why do I need a scout? I can follow a straight, abandoned road. I'll hit Medahon, then it's a lovely journey to the City of Reckoning. Nick can't be that far ahead."

She wished her brothers were here, making jokes. She wished Mom were here, stroking her hair. She missed them all.

"Chloe."

Chloe jumped to her feet. A girl stood in the lovely meadow opposite the direction Scout had gone.

A girl. Just a girl like me. Chloe's heartbeat slowed and she smiled. *Well, not quite like me.*

Precious stones adorned the visitor's dress and sparkled in the sunlight. She was a princess. Or an angel. Chloe peeked down at her own dingy clothes, the same clothes she'd been wearing since her arrival.

Chloe swallowed and pulled her T-shirt to hide the bottom of her scar.

"I bet you're lonely," the girl said.

Don't speak. Don't speak.

"Walk with me." The girl smiled and backed off the road. She was so beautiful — more so than any movie star who'd ever appeared on Aldo's screen. Chloe stepped forward, and then again.

"Stay on the road!"

The voice was urgent, distant, and Chloe ignored it. Another step, and her toe brushed the grass.

"A little farther." The beautiful one stared at Chloe's feet.

"She's not a girl!" Scout screamed.

Chloe blinked hard and staggered back. The girl's face snarled, darkened, shrunk. A beak grew and wings spread, and a hideous buzzard took off toward the east.

Scout slumped back onto the road.

"What did you say?"

"Uh ... nothing. I ... I said nothing."

Scout frowned. "Then why did it come? What were you doing when you first saw her?"

Chloe mentally retraced her steps. "Thinking of home."

"Memories," Scout whispered. "The Senseri are drawn to your memories. Understand this: any Retinyan man or beast that turns, that sides with Vaepor, will, like It, start to lose its own shape to take on other forms. Do not trust any appearance you see. Only when anxious do Senseri lapse back to who they really are."

Chloe's face was blank.

Scout stepped nearer. "I do not know what men fight for in your world. But here, the battle is for our thoughts, our memories. It wants them. It's scared of them. For no free-thinking man will follow It." He breathed deeply. "So as long as you didn't speak, as long as you stayed on the road, the Senseri saw your scar and likely thought you just another Lost One. It might suspect, but it doesn't know."

"Know what?"

"I'm not sure. But for a Senseri to stray so far from the palace, you're more valuable than I'd imagined."

Chloe bit her lip and winced. "My foot did brush grass—"

Scout's eyes widened and he grabbed her arm. "Then we run."

They ran east, following the path of the bird.

Between rapid breaths, Scout said, "They know visitors have broken through. They know of your friend. They will come for you. We need to reach Medahon."

ON THEY RAN, until Chloe's thighs stung and her lungs ached, and then, suddenly, they didn't hurt at all. The second wind she usually experienced in the 800-meter breaststroke wafted over her, and her pace quickened. But it soon disappeared, and she slowed to a limp beside Scout.

"I can't, Scout. I need to rest for —"

Chloe's toe caught on cobblestone, and she collapsed on the road. Scout bent over and gently lifted her to her feet.

"There."

Lights burned brightly, and even from a distance, Medahon loomed, a great fortress city with jagged walls poking into the sky.

"We'll make it," Scout said. "Just a couple miles, and —"

"And then what? You'll leave me too?"

Scout exhaled hard and grabbed her hand. "No. I can no longer leave." His face was grim. "I think your business and my business might be one and the same."

A horn blared. Not a sharp trumpet call, but a moaning roar. For minutes, it filled the air with sadness, and then it stopped — at least Chloe thought it did. The tone roared on inside her brain.

"What was that?"

"The Call. Tomorrow the Pilgrimage begins. The dark march to the pool will start, and the entire city will empty."

"Oh, I wish I didn't have to see this."

Scout raised his eyebrows. "Yes, but understand what is horrible for Retinya is in this case good for you. Medahon will be in panicked preparation for the morning's departure. In the chaos, you will be hard to find." He glanced at the sky. "That is, if we can get into the city before the gates close."

"Then please, let's go!" Chloe said.

Filled with new strength, they pushed forward toward granite walls, which closer up were only taller and more imposing.

I never meant to write them this big.

"The walls of Medahon." Scout huffed. "They

withstood many attacks. But now men have forgotten why they fought."

An unnatural shadow spread over them quickly, turning day to night. Chloe slowed to glance up, but Scout grasped her arm and quickened the pace. A thunderclap rippled through the cloud that eclipsed the city and lightning jagged across the darkening sky. Greenish funnels swirled overhead, but on the ground there was barely a breeze.

"It's going to pour," Chloe said.

"That's no storm cloud." Scout released her arm. "That's Vaepor. Watching. Waiting."

Chloe looked up, stumbled, and regained her balance. "Waiting for ..."

"You."

From behind came the clop of horses' hooves. A herd of fifty overtook them and slowed. On the back of each horse was a musician, and on the back of each musician was a pack bulging with musical instruments. Wild, colorful strips of clothing formed turbans on the riders' heads, and they bowed low and hopped off their mounts. Chloe pressed into Scout as tambourines, flutes, and horns filled the air with loud, excruciating noise. It sounded like an off-key band, except far more painful. The troop danced, flailing and whooping with each gyration.

"They're all drunk," Chloe said. "Just like Dad's workers."

Scout again grabbed her hand and pulled her into their circle. "We're in luck. Calainic gypsies. And no, they haven't been drinking!" He grinned. "See the scars?"

Children, grown-ups, and all ages between bore deep marks on their faces and necks.

Chloe nodded. *Even the kids go into the pool?*

Gypsy children grasped hands and ringed Chloe, circling and giggling. *Life without memories doesn't look so bad.* They sure seemed carefree.

"Dance!" Scout rolled his eyes and spun in a limping circle. "We'll need cover to enter the gates." As soon as the words left his lips, another violent thunderclap came from above. "Come on, Chloe. Join!"

There was no pattern to the craziness. Chloe jumped and flung her arms, hoping she fit in.

Grandpa would love this.

The more Chloe jumped, the lighter she felt. She couldn't remember the last time she'd leaped or shouted. Not in this world. Certainly not in her own world. In swim meets, she felt wild freedom, but only when underwater, and there strokes required focused discipline. She certainly didn't feel this light in Aldo's projection booth, where she couldn't do much more than whisper.

Chloe suddenly felt a vibration. She glanced at the pale, blue light coming from her pocket.

Scout's eyes widened, and he rushed toward her. "What were you doing?"

"Nothing!" She plastered her hands over the glow, but again light penetrated her fingers. "Just thinking I couldn't remember dancing like this before."

"Remembering. Figures." He leaned over. "It might be wise to keep your mind in this world until we're in the city."

Scout glanced around then froze. A dark, twisting finger descended from above. It reached the cobblestones and bent forward, like a widening funnel. Out from the spinning darkness strode a tall, robed man, nine, maybe ten feet tall. Travelers parted in front of him, and his eyes glowed the same color as Chloe's stone.

"Vaepor's found you." Scout stepped between the man and Chloe and hobbled forward. The music stopped. In fact, everything stopped but the roar from above. Chloe ducked behind a harpist ten feet behind Scout.

"I don't want to speak with you, brave fool," the robed man croaked. "Stand aside. I will speak with the girl."

"No, you will not!" Scout's voice rang out in the silence.

The man raised his hand, and with a movement so quick Chloe barely followed it, crunched his fist into Scout's ribs. His hand entered Scout's body and appeared out his back.

"Scout!" screamed Chloe.

But Chloe's protector was not moved. He grabbed the shoulder of the giant and flung him backward, where the man stared gape-jawed at his own clenched fingers.

Scout stepped nearer. "You are hollow! You have no memory. You don't know who you are. You can't hurt me." Scout's voice strengthened. "And you may not touch her!"

Scout spun and forced both his hands into the giant's midsection. "Change!"

The giant recoiled and gave a hideous scream. His form shifted and grew into a creature much like Flit, except no bird features — including the soft underfeathers — remained. It was 100 percent dragon, with a scarred and burned underbelly. The dragon scooped up Scout with his talons and slowly lifted him from the ground.

"I'll come to you," Scout shouted down. "Leave

the city with nobody else. Don't even leave with me, unless you're sure!"

"Scout!" Chloe cried, and chased the dragon until it disappeared behind the city walls. The music and dancing returned, but Chloe could not join. Not anymore.

First Nick, then Nob, and now Scout. Everyone's leaving me!

"Don't cry." A kind-looking woman gave her a hug. "Dance. Soon we'll all be free from these painful memories. When we reach that glorious pool!"

"No!" Chloe pulled away and stumbled forward. *I don't even know who you are!*

The stone in her pocket felt heavy, but its glow had faded. "Dumb rock. You're what Vaepor saw. I should throw you away ..."

She'd reached the gate — doors two stories high and built of solid wood, which she'd created as the only entrance into a fortress city with walls of fitted stone. And there, sitting by the entrance, leaning back against the rock wall, was Nick.

Musicians shouted and danced all the wilder as Chloe pushed her way to his side of the street.

"Nick!"

He cocked his head and stood, scanning the group of gypsies. Chloe relaxed.

We'll leave the city together. I can remember enough to get us to the palace. Scout's face floated into her mind, but she shook the image out. *I can't help him now. I have to get through the window and home. Secholit will have to help Retinya remember by himself.*

Chloe opened her mouth to call to her friend, but let it flap shut.

Another Nick, identical to the first, wandered aimlessly just inside the gate. "I'm lost! I'm lost! Chloe, help me."

Then another appeared, and another. The entire entrance teemed with Nicks. Identical, and searching.

"Nothing is as it seems," Chloe whispered.

Senseri.

The first Nick stepped into the crowd of dancers. "Chloe? Was that you? I can't believe you found me!"

Chloe glanced wildly around, and danced. She grabbed a flute from the woman beside her and blew a note, loud and ugly. She tried to squeeze to the edge of the road, but bodies funneled toward the gate and pushed her right in front of—

"Oof!"

Nick and Chloe collided, and she fell to the cobblestones. Nick leaned over, grabbed Chloe's hand, and helped her to her feet. He paused and she paused, and for a moment everything else vanished. Nick scanned her, searched her. His head cocked and he reached out and touched the scar, rolled his eyes, and kept walking. "Chloe? Have any of you seen a girl with that name?"

Chloe exhaled, and danced a furious dance into the city — she didn't stop until all the look-alikes were behind her.

I need to find Scout.

She pressed deeper into Medahon and stilled. Aldo would have loved this city when it was first built — the buildings were straight out of a Salvador Dali painting or a Dr. Seuss book. Chloe imagined how it would have looked long ago: Rooms perched on pedestals, walkways rose, fell, and vanished. And the stairs! They twisted and wound, one even looping like an out-of-control roller coaster. A few climbed into the sky, disappearing into the dark, rumbling cloud.

But the city had crumbled, as if shaken by a giant earthquake. Chunks of stone lay exploded on the ground, buildings were riddled with holes, and the walls — labyrinth-filled and once beautiful — were cracked and crumbling.

Chloe walked on, and the road widened and

spread into an enormous courtyard dotted with thousands of identical gray tents, with thousands of people milling in all directions.

"I'll never find the real him," Chloe muttered. "Grandpa, what would you do?"

Immediately, her stone blazed blue. Those nearest her shielded their eyes from the light.

"I see you, Chloe!" Vaepor descended, and voices changed to screams. Out of his cloud screeched five creatures like the one who had taken Scout.

"Quiet, you dumb stone!"

Chloe leaped into a tent, where a family reclined around a picnic that smelled of fried chicken. The littlest girl scampered into her mother's arms, and Chloe snatched up her drumstick.

"I'm sorry! I just need to be in a tent right now. And after three days of lingonberries ..."

She dug in her pocket and pulled out the stone, then dropped to her knees, stuck the drumstick in her teeth, and scratched at the soft earth like a dog. *I'm going to bury you. I'm sick of being chased every time I remember something.*

She paused and scanned her surroundings. A whisper of vapor flicked in beneath the canvas, and the tent lifted skyward. Chloe pocketed the rock and ran. "If I don't die first!"

Chloe weaved through the chaos. Creatures from above swooped and grabbed and ripped at the surrounding tents, filling the air with parachuting canvas. Tent pegs and dragon talons and children's screams mixed together in a hideous scene, and Chloe froze.

"Hello, Chloe."

"Nick?" The voice was his, but the figure was Vaepor's. The swirling mass surrounded her, billowing nearer on all sides. "Did they tell you I was painful? That was a lie."

Chloe glanced around. Only two tents remained in her shrinking circle.

"Did they tell you I was evil? That was a lie too."

That's it. I'm going to die.

"Don't be afraid. I alone can send you back home. As you saw, and as you now hear, our friend Nick already knows that." Vaepor collapsed in on Chloe, just as strong hands grabbed her by the shoulder and yanked her inside the last tent.

"Enjoy the ride, young one. Greet Quill for me."

The next feeling was that of falling, and then coasting like she was on the waterslide at the Melmanie pool. But there was no water; just a smooth stone slope that had no end.

She slid so deep and for so long, Chloe forgot the

fate she'd narrowly escaped. Her mind wandered home, to horses and chickens and quiet country roads. Minnesota was beautiful.

Chloe sped around a sharp corner and felt her speed ease. She pressed her hands against the inside of the stone chute and slowed to a stop. When she jumped to her feet, the room around her spun, and she toppled onto her knees. Chloe closed her eyes tightly, waited for her world to still, and cracked open an eyelid.

"Please, please be the Quints."

15

CHLOE STOOD IN A CHAMBER deep underground. It was well lit, though Chloe could see no lanterns, and was far too beautiful to be a cave. The room's walls were decorated with portraits, top to bottom, of families and parties and holiday get-togethers.

I've fallen into a photo album.

Chloe's stone glowed, but the brightness around her swallowed up its light. She stepped forward, and only then looked up.

Stairs — at least the bottom eight steps of a stair-case — hung down through the ceiling like an icicle from a roof.

"Never seen you the roots of a stairs before? Hmm?"

"Actually, I have. In my dreams. In a room exactly like this." Chloe slowly turned and smiled.

Yes! I've found the Quints!

Before her stood the oldest, kindest face she'd ever met. Shorter than a full-sized man, bald as a bowling ball, and talk about old — his wrinkles were deep as caverns. The man's shirt and trousers strained to contain his stocky frame. He was a friend. Chloe knew this the moment she saw him.

He laughed, and the sound filled the hall. "I'm pleased to hear your dreams are giving you the education school does not."

School. Chloe rubbed her face and tried to remember it. It seemed so far away. "In class we learn the latitude of Fiji, the proper way to factor a trinomial, the history of the United States ... really important stuff."

His hand shot out and covered her mouth. "The past is worth your attention. If you can read it, there's a good chance you should." He peered to his left. Chloe followed his glance and her jaw dropped. Bookshelves lined an entire wall and continued on until the room jogged left far in the distance.

"These books weren't in my dream. Have you read them all?"

"Not yet. But with fortune, there'll be time."

Chloe walked to the nearest shelf and pulled out a volume. "*The War of the Eristad.* Never heard of it."

"That is because it wasn't fought in your world. Follow me. We must get you fed, as you have much to do."

He reached out his hand.

Don't leave here without me. Scout's warning echoed, and she stared at the stout man's fingers.

"Yes," her host said, "Scout would approve of this."

"How did you know …" Chloe smiled. "Never-mind." She grabbed the Quint's hand, and together they moved through the chamber.

"You're wondering about the pictures. They are taken up above, in the city. We do all we can to capture as many families as we can. We record lives, in book as well as in photo." He sighed. "At march's end, they'll forget. We'll hold the last record of who is whose."

"A hall of memories," she whispered.

"Put well." He straightened. "And now prepare to meet the other Quints. Qujan, especially, has been eager to greet you. Oh, forgive me — my name! Please call me Quill."

"Quill the Quint." She laughed. "Oh, I'm sorry, that just sounded funny to me."

"Laugh away, young one. Your road gets harder from here."

Chloe later tried to describe the home of the Quints, but was scarcely able to remember the particulars, which is odd as it was a chamber filled with memories. She had no problem recalling dinner, however. Lamb and salmon and cake — chocolate, to be exact.

Quill sat beside her at one of the tables that filled the dining hall. Surrounding them were fifty, maybe sixty other Quints, each nearly identical in appearance to Quill. Except for hair; Quill was the only bald one among them. Chloe quickly discovered that Quints were messy eaters — much like Q back home. Fully half of their food tumbled and dripped down their shirts.

But the most memorable things in that room were the tables. Simple picnic tables — the kind that filled her own dining room — stretched across the space, and joyful conversation surrounded each one. It was the sound of home. Even with a stressed mom and a crazy dad and wild brothers and Grandpa Salvador, Chloe's house was Italian-loud and cheerful at mealtimes. In those moments, she felt she had family.

The Quints laughed and hooted and ate. Inside, Chloe felt warm. Yes, she decided, if she never returned home, life with the Quints would be an acceptable alternative. So much nicer than the elves' darkness.

"No, Chloe," Quill whispered. "You can't stay here, not even one night. You're needed above."

"But ever since Nick and I began working on the — I mean, I've been hoping I'd run into you since I got here."

"So famous we are in all worlds! This is good news, yet hardly unexpected." He motioned to a Quint seated at the end of the table. "Her book, please."

The small man rose and left the room. Minutes later, he returned, bowed, and handed Chloe a thick volume.

She frowned, pushed aside her plate, and opened to page one.

Pictures of me? How did you get these?

"You imagine you are the only one from your family to eat at this table?"

She looked up slowly. Something in her knew.

"Grandpa?"

Quill peeked at the female Quint seated on Chloe's left. She was craning her neck to see the photographs, but quickly blushed and leaned back on the bench. Quill raised his eyebrows and gestured for her to speak.

"My name is Qujan. Yes, my dear Salvador, and before him — "

"Aldo," Chloe whispered.

Qujan smiled at his name. "Yes, Salvador's very handsome father, as you see further on."

Chloe spent the next hour poring over family photographs. Until Dad's face appeared sprinkled among the pictures. "I don't want to see these anymore."

"That may work with elves, but not here." Quill tapped her book. "Learn."

Chloe forced down her gaze. It was the same image she'd seen in the blue mirror — a crying father — but this time she clearly saw his hand, and in it a picture of her before the accident.

"Grandpa wasn't here recently. How do you have photos of me?"

"The photos filled in the moment you arrived," Qujan said. "You brought memories with you. See, see the way your father weeps?"

"He doesn't look at me." Chloe pointed at her chin. "He can't after this hideous thing ..." She broke into tears.

"Turn the page," Quill said softly.

"No."

"I can't turn it for you. Turn the page."

Chloe wiped the tears with the heel of her hand and obeyed. The page held only one photo. It was of her, and she was beautiful. The scar was there, but though she tried she couldn't focus on the imper-fection. Her face was radiant, triumphant. But there was no background in the photo. Just Chloe.

"I don't look like this. Where was this taken?"

Quill reached over and closed the book. "It's a memory that has not yet been made."

"Oh, will it happen? I was beautiful ... I mean, I looked like I *felt* beautiful."

Qujan leaned over. "You alone can make that memory. It's not out of reach."

Chloe stroked her scar and felt a searing inside. *Not possible.*

"Family?" Quill rumbled and every Quint jumped up. "We must see that Chloe reaches the uppermost floor. If one of Pindle's children grabbed Scout, that is where he'll be. I've not called on you since Aldo's day, but now a greater evil wishes to stop Chloe's search before it begins. She'll need Scout if she is to survive the march."

"No." Chloe's head thumped down onto the table. "I don't want to hear any more about surviving. You showed me my family, and now I want Nick and a way home."

"I'm afraid that Nick is home." Quill stared at Chloe. "His album is black."

Chloe raised her head. "What does that mean?"

"Listen, Chloe, for now you must forget Nick. If you see him, it will likely not be him in flesh. And Nob has fled, I cannot see where. Above, in the city, you and Scout will be alone. But you will have another companion as well; you have your memories. Be aware you will be watched not only by the Senseri, but also by many things good, and that is a comforting thought. Find Scout, march toward the pool, and finish the quest you were wounded to complete."

Chloe looked around the table. "Does anyone here understand what he just said?"

"Forget Nick. Find Scout. To the pool." Qujan slapped Quill with the back of her hand. "Males can be so complicated."

A train of Quints instantly rose and led Chloe to the Great Hall.

Quill cracked thick knuckles. "Quall, start the chain."

A LARGE QUINT Chloe assumed had to be Quall lay down and raised his hands toward the ceiling. Another Quint lay on the first.

"I don't mean to complain." Quall glanced at Quill. "But I did start the last chain."

"And you'll start the next one too."

Quint after Quint added to the living ladder until twenty-one Quints formed stumpy but shaky rungs stretching from the floor to the root of the stairs.

Quall, arms shaking, turned his head to one side. "I don't mean to rush you, but it is a bit heavy."

"Rush *me*?" Chloe slowly shook her head backed away.

"Climb these stairs, Chloe." Quill eased her toward the pile of Quints. "It will lead you nowhere, which is exactly where you'll find Scout. According to Quist, who located you in Tent City, dragons circle without ceasing on the eve of the terrible Pilgrimage. But Vaepor has vanished from the skies, leading me to believe It thinks it has found the greater prize: your Nick. But It is wrong." He removed a volume from his bookshelf. "I believe Scout is still alive. His pictures still shine, although not brightly. Senseri will be roaming the streets waiting for you to rescue him."

"So, you want me to save Scout from some dragons and a villainous cloud?" Chloe shouted. "I don't know how." She lowered her voice. "I'm not that brave."

"Oh, Chloe, you are. Do not lose the mountain stone, as it may yet serve you well, and to it I add my gift." Quill handed her the picture, the beautiful one. "When you wonder who you truly are, look and see. And may you find this memory."

"If it's no bother," Quall grunted, "could we start soon?"

Chloe winced and scampered onto his belly.

"Quill." Qujan grabbed his arm. "It may be time to surface. While we cower, the land above falls. When has Retinya been in greater need?"

"Cower? We do our part from below, Qujan.

Retinya is not the only world that needs our aid. You should know this most of all. We do not involve ourselves directly in the affairs of men when — "

Qujan glared and raised her hands to her hips. "This is not what you told me when Salvador was in need."

"That was different." Quill rubbed his forehead and lowered his voice. "He's family."

"And what does that make Chloe?"

Chloe paused with her knee pressed against a Quint's hand. "Please, I don't know what you're talking about. But if you can help …"

Quill raised both arms toward the ceiling. "Enough. I will consider your request, Qujan. Were you not my daughter, I would discipline you."

"Then it's a good thing I am." Qujan turned to Chloe. "Climb, and do not fear." She winked. "You have not seen the last of us yet."

Chloe stepped up. "Don't run," Quall said, and Chloe climbed higher.

"Don't run." The next Quint whispered as she stepped. "Don't run."

"Don't run."

"Don't run."

"Don't run."

Chloe scrambled onto the last Quint and reached

for the stairs' bottom step. "I know, I know." She chuckled. "Don't run."

He stared sadly into Chloe's eyes. "From your father."

Chloe paused, then continued onto the staircase, turning just in time to see the Quints tumble onto the floor. From somewhere within the pile, Quall groaned, "There must be an easier way to do that."

She laughed and breathed deeply. "Don't run from your father. Give up on Nick. Find Scout in Medahon, where everyone is after me on a set of stairs going nowhere. Sure, why not?"

Chloe climbed through the ceiling, and immediately all light from below disappeared.

"No, no. I can't climb in the dark." She paused. "Don't run from your father. My father, Crazy Ray." She giggled as she remembered the airplane he built for squirrels. He had tethered it to the chicken coop to scare away hawks. Oh, the hissing those squirrels made. The invention worked for a week ... until Q shot all the rodent pilots.

As she thought, her stone lit up the stairway.

Memory light. Just what I need.

"Don't run from my father? Okay, but just on these stairs."

At first, Chloe passed time counting steps. But

as her legs numbed, her mind wandered and she lost track — and balance. It wasn't the number of steps, but their depth. They followed no consistent pattern. A wide, comfortable step followed a narrow, shallow one barely deep enough to support a toe.

The shaft around her was no more forgiving. Broad and angular, its walls were out of Chloe's reach. Occasionally, railing remnants provided handholds, but for the most part she climbed through silent, empty space.

And then, voices. They were muffled at first, but with each step they became louder and clearer until she turned a corner, saw firelight above, and climbed into a night filled with torchlight.

Medahon.

Chloe quickly pocketed her stone and raised her gaze. The stairway continued its rickety spiral skyward until it disappeared into dense fog. Around her, deep voices filled the square.

Senseri wander the streets. Keep going, Chloe!

She quickly found the journey toward the clouds a much more frightening climb. Similar to the underground section, there were few railings, but unlike the portion below, the stairway creaked and swayed in the stiff breeze.

Chloe peeked down and felt her head lighten.

"Quints are at the bottom of this. I could ease back down and get a good meal and a good night's sleep."

A gust rocked the stairway and Chloe dropped to her knees. She crawled upward until her body could go no farther.

This was because there were no more steps to take. The stairway simply ended. At this altitude, the fog cleared, and the lights of the city spread out below. Staircases of equally dizzying heights reached into space around her, some ending nowhere, some leading into rooms or disappearing into large nests.

"You've come back."

That voice — the same thick, throaty rasp that had come from the robed man who attacked Scout. Chloe turned and started back down, until a rush of wind almost sent her tumbling off the stairway. A scarred dragon descended and flapped, snout to Chloe's eyeballs. It circled the swaying staircase.

"What's a girl like you doing way up here? You seem out of place."

Four more dragons screeched down from the sky. They rushed toward the staircase, biting and clawing each other as they came. One surged ahead and wrapped a talon around Chloe's waist.

"My prize! I'll be giving her to Vaepor when he returns tomorrow."

Chloe screamed, and up they flew. "No, please!" But her shriek was lost in the flap of wings. Minutes later, the creature set her in its nest, pinning her between its weighty wing and the dead branches beneath.

"Why do you need me?" Chloe struggled. "Why—"

"Shh," it said. "Your memory truly is short."

"Flit!"

Feathers engulfed her. The dragon tucked its head beneath its wing and exhaled a long, warm blast of air. "Scout is beneath one of the others. No doubt much less comfortable. We don't have much time before Vaepor arrives. Be ready when I signal."

Chloe nestled into Flit's soft feathers. They felt like her bed back home, and slowly she drifted to sleep.

CHAPTER

17

"COME, CHILD."

Chloe left her dream and hurtled through the sky. Flit's talon drew her deeper into his feathers, and she pressed against his warm body. Flit circled high above Medahon, finally alighting on the edge of another nest. Chloe swept large feathers from her face and strained her neck forward to see through the thick mass of fluff.

"Get up, Yizash." Flit slapped the sleeping dragon across the face.

The creature slowly cracked an eyelid. "Away with you, feathered one."

Flit hopped to the other side of the nest, balancing on one talon. "You stole my human. I want the girl back. You already have your prize."

"All I have is the lame boy." Yizash closed her eye. "I caught him fair, at considerable pain to me."

"And it clearly wasn't enough for you." Flit slapped her again. This time Yizash rose.

"If you strike me again …"

Flit bent over the smaller dragon. "I'll do more than that, sister, if you don't hand her over."

Yizash's great eyes narrowed. She drew her body up, slowly beat her wings, and lifted into the night sky. There she hovered, her eyes fixed on Flit. "The human has been anguish to me all night."

In the bottom of the nest lay Scout, curled up with eyes open wide.

"As you see. Just the boy."

Flit stretched forward and his body tensed. Chloe's did too. "Yes," Flit whispered, "just the boy."

Flit launched, ducked beneath Yizash, snatched Scout, and dived toward the city, all in one smooth stroke. Behind him, Yizash gave a hideous shriek, and within moments more shrieks filled the air. Flit missled straight down, gaining speed. Chloe braced and watched Medahon's lights fast approach, but she felt no fear. She sensed what was coming.

Whoosh! Flit skimmed the street and wove between buildings at tremendous speed before spinning to the right, where he released her and Scout an arm's length from the inside of the wall.

"Into the crack!" With that Flit and his words quickly disappeared.

Scout grabbed Chloe's hand and yanked her into a crumbled gap between loose wall stones. She landed on her backside and tucked in her legs, rolling forward as four dragons screeched by. She and Scout lay motionless, side by side, until the sound of dragons vanished in the distance. Chloe's breathing slowed, and she propped herself up on an elbow.

"What just happened? Oh, Scout, I didn't think I'd ever find you. I mean, there were thirty Nicks and I ran for the tents and then a Quint — have you ever seen a Quint? — saved me from — "

"Stop," he said. "Are you sure it's me?"

Chloe squinted hard. "Well, yeah, I think — Oh. I don't know anything."

Scout smiled and sat up. "Ask me something only I would know. Something you told me in private."

She frowned. "When I first met you, you told me something — "

Scout thought a minute. "Don't stray to the left or to the right. The ground is evil." He winked. "At least most of it."

Chloe hugged him. She couldn't help it. But Scout pried her loose.

"But the Quint line is gone. They are no more. Whoever told you of them is filled with wishful thinking. Clearly, your day's been hard. Now sleep," he said, his face haggard. "We should be safe here tonight. Tomorrow we take to the Path, where Vaepor will be watching. It may already have Nick, and if so you become Its desire. But that's a worry for a different day. Tonight, rest easy. I'll watch."

Chloe pressed deeper into the wall and found a nook where she could stretch her legs. *The Quints didn't seem gone. Maybe I am crazy.* As she settled in to sleep, Scout sat and hummed. A song she'd heard somewhere in a different world.

• • •

Drumbeats.

Chloe woke to drumbeats.

"Time to leave," Scout said.

She yawned and stepped out from the wall. She'd seen Medahon at night and beneath Vaepor's cloud, but it looked quite different in the light of day, filled with color and song and smile and song.

"They look happy to begin the trip," Chloe said.

Scout was quiet.

"Did I say something wrong?"

He paused. "They are happy — happy and deceived."

Chloe and Scout pressed into the crowd exiting out a back gate Chloe didn't remember creating. There, the road widened, and the cobblestones had been sanded smooth. As Chloe set foot outside the town, her face brightened.

"A carnival!"

On both sides of the broad, one-way road, street vendors handed treats to children. The smells and colors were irresistible. Chloe ran from booth to booth, and then skipped back to Scout.

"Brownie-like things and doughnut-shaped stuff right over there!" She held up a chewy cookie. "And it's all free!"

"It's not what it seems." Scout tipped his head and focused on a point farther down the road.

Chloe followed Scout's gaze to an old man hobbling alone. He seemed out of place as he fought his way back against the sweep of the crowd.

"I saw him before I was taken away." Scout bent to her ear. "No scar. That man has all his memories, and from the looks of things, he doesn't want to lose them."

The man reached the edge of the road, looked both ways, and slipped between two booths. When he emerged he ran straight toward the city. The drumbeat quickened, and two giggling children directly in front of Chloe released their balloons and sprinted after him. The moment they stepped off the road, their bodies morphed into strong young men. They quickly caught up with the gentleman, struck his back, spun him around, and hoisted him onto their shoulders.

"Escorts," Scout whispered. "Senseri in training. A good reason to keep our voices low."

"Why are they so cruel?"

"They dread that man. He knows who he is, and isn't afraid of his pain. He also knows how evil they are."

Chloe glanced back and the three were gone. Scout gestured toward the booths. "They function like a fence. Once you start on this path, there's no way off."

She stared at her cookie and dropped it to the road. She used the free hand to grab Scout's neckline and pull his head down. "Then what are *we* doing here?"

Scout straightened and flattened his shirt. "Nick. We need to follow. He could be right in front of us."

"No, he couldn't. The elves said the trees set him down in the river."

"Which he hates. He would quickly disembark, head for the easy road."

Forget about Nick. Find Scout. March toward the pool and don't run from your father—

There was no use bringing Qujan's words into the argument, not with Scout. Silence fell, and Chloe searched for words to fill the space.

"Scout, tell me about your family."

He said nothing.

"Can I ask you ... is your father still alive?"

Scout's face twitched. "Yes."

"Does it hurt you to speak about him?"

"Yes."

I sure get that. "Does he ever hurt you ... I mean, the way he acts ... Is he proud of you?"

"My father gave me this." He rubbed his limping leg.

Chloe's eyes widened, and she rubbed her neck. "My dad gave me this! Tell me about your accident."

"The only accident was he didn't strike me higher up, through the heart."

Chloe winced.

Scout grabbed her arm. "Do not place our fathers in the same sentence. I know of your father. What happened was tragic, but it came from love, his desire to share his discovery—"

"How do you know —"

"I told you, I have been many places. Your father took nothing from you. Strength, beauty, it's all still there. My father took my usefulness. My father took my speed. An able-limbed guide might have fought off Vaepor, might have reached Nick before he set off." Scout's fingers squeezed so hard, Chloe's arm ached. "When your father attempts to run you through with his staff, we will have something to talk about."

Scout released Chloe's arm and turned away.

Chloe massaged her muscle and whispered quietly, "Okay, you know what? Let's avoid family small talk for now." She breathed deeply. "And maybe, since Nick doesn't mind being on his own, we should let Nick go too — for now, I mean. Let's just get to the pool …" Chloe's voice dropped away. No matter what the Quints said, leaving Nick didn't feel right. *Don't let him go, Chloe.* Wasn't that what Grandpa Salvador said?

Scout furrowed his eyebrows. "We should find Nick first. Always, Nick first." He thought and nodded. "Let's try something. Keep walking." Scout left Chloe's side and pushed into the middle of the street. And from his direction, a chant began to the drum's steady beat.

"Nick. Nick. Nick."

Others joined in, and Scout scooted to another group. They, too, took up the chant.

"Nick. Nick."

Those around Chloe erupted in the one-word chorus. "Nick. Nick. Nick. Nick."

Hundreds turned to thousands. The tent vendors stared at each other, shrugged, and joined in.

The chant was so loud that it quickly overshadowed the drums. The noise was so intense, in fact, Chloe barely noticed when Scout returned to her side and said, "There. That will bring It."

"It? The Vaepor thing? I don't want It here!" She paused. "And how did you get them to say that?"

Scout shrugged. "If you've forgotten what's normal and good, you'll do anything."

The sky darkened as a shadow stretched over the road. Scout's lips tightened. "Vaepor."

The shadow slowly covered the land, changing blue sky to murky gray. The air weighed down on Chloe and breathing became difficult. "How could anybody want to follow that hideous cloud?"

"That fact, dear Chloe, has saved this land more than once. If Vaepor had an appealing form, I fear every human would already be under Its control."

Thunder clapped, but the thunder had a voice. Deep, clear, foreboding. "Silence."

The road fell quiet except for the cries of children. Even the drumbeat stopped, though it pounded on inside Chloe's head.

"I heard your calls for Nick. You all would like to see him again. And you will." Vaepor gathered, thickened, and then rolled over the road. Men gasped and cowered. "At the pool, you will hear Nick Secholit speak. There, do exactly as he says."

Vaepor spun into a funnel cloud, and, with a roar that knocked Scout and Chloe to their knees, vanished toward the east.

The drumbeat began and the march resumed.

"That was Vaepor? And what did he mean?"

"I don't know. Nick Secholit? It makes no sense." Scout rubbed his face, hard. "I do believe It's found Nick, and if so, Nick is beginning to change. I'm too late. I arrived too late."

Chloe stood, and a large man collided with her back. She regained her balance and the sea of marchers parted around the pair. "You mean we're both too late."

Scout closed his eyes and shook his head. "This was my job." He grabbed her arm and pulled her forward. "Don't stop. It draws attention." He puffed out air as they plodded with the crowd. "We're of no use to him now." Scout appeared to drift into thought for a minute. "But you already knew that. You just told me. How did you know he was lost?"

Chloe glanced down. "I know a lot of things about this place. But about Nick ... There's something else I need to do before I find him, that's all. I'm not quitting on him. I won't leave him here."

"Who said quit?" Scout grimaced. "But if Nick's already with Vaepor, we'll need lots of help, and I fear I've led you astray. Now you're stuck on a dangerous path." He bumped her shoulder. "But you can't quit, not if Secholit gave you a task. And remember, glorious failures are often much more wonderful than easy victories."

Losing your friend sure doesn't feel glorious.

CHAPTER

18

They walked the rest of the day in silence. By evening, all that remained in Chloe's head was the constant drumbeat. Steady. Always steady. The entire procession marched in step to that unnatural drum, all except for Scout. Chloe tried to break free from the beat, but her feet quickly fell back into the easy rhythm.

Finally, the drumbeat slowed, and the march stopped. The travelers had reached a bulge in the road. It resembled a huge cul-de-sac, except the road continued out the other end. But with the urging thump gone, the entire parade spread out blankets and lay down on the cobbled street. Minstrels wandered among them playing soft, sleepy music.

"There are ten of these stops," Scout said. "Ten days of walking until we reach the City of Reckoning, through which runs the only road to the pool."

Chloe nodded. Suddenly she was very tired and lay down, her back cool against the smooth stones. "Are you serious? We're ten days from this pool? Nobody will leave the road for *ten days*?"

"They widened it to make us comfortable. People have no reason to leave." He paused. "What are you thinking about?"

Chloe propped herself up on an elbow. "We can't stay on this road for half that long. We're too visible. I've already bumped into Vaepor three times. We're going to get off, no matter what it takes." She glanced at his leg. "How well do you swim?"

"Not my strong suit, actually," Scout whispered, and gave Chloe a sideways glance. "No, Chloe. No, and no. The lake is not an option. Escorts line the road across its entire span."

Chloe barely held back a grin. "Okay, not a lake."

The next morning carried the feeling of a camping trip. As she stretched and wiped the sleep from her eyes, Chloe held on to a dream about Mom and Dad and an autumn trail ride, back when Dad's eyes sparkled and his hugs felt big and safe. Dad hadn't invaded her dreams for years.

She and Scout rose and joined the other pilgrims marching down the road. As the day grew long, the procession broke up, with older folks falling toward the back and younger couples and families taking the lead. Chloe and Scout's limp settled into the drumbeat's pace somewhere in between.

Scout's limp was more pronounced. Chloe watched him grimace, and the words fell out.

"Why did your dad do it?"

He breathed deeply. "I was injured in battle."

"Battle?" she gasped. "You're too young to be in a battle."

Scout glanced at her. "Everyone is, but battles come anyway."

Boom. Boom.

Burble.

The thumping so filled her brain, it was hard to focus on Scout's voice, much less a tiny gurgling. But the sound was unmistakable. Water flowed ahead.

"You'll do better if you kick off your shoes." Chloe said. "I knew we'd cross this soon."

Scout leaned in. "I don't understand."

Their pace slowed as thousands of people bottle-necked, squeezing forward on the thinning road.

"Ah, the short bridge." Scout jostled about as the crowd converged. "The most uncomfortable ten seconds of the entire trip. Everyone squeezes across it."

"We won't."

"We won't?"

The river's babbling turned rushing torrent. Chloe pressed her way onto the bridge and surged forward, carried by the tide of pilgrims at her back.

"Listen, Vaepor's looking for us here. I say we swim up the Green River, follow its bank through the Northern Mountains, cross the Safelands, find a way across the bay to Shadowton, and pick the road up right there. It's more a longcut than a shortcut, but maybe safer, right?"

Scout's face was blank. "And this knowledge of Retinyan geography comes from ..."

"Algebra. That's mainly where I drew the maps."

"Right." Scout cleared his throat. "May I simply tell you that a successful traverse by your route exists somewhere between crazy and impossible?"

Chloe nodded. "Crazy and impossible." She bit her lip and thought. "Which one is it closer to?"

"It is ... it is both!" He shrugged his shoulders. "Hear your history. You followed the girl onto the grass, not heeding my warning. You now wish to journey where tragedy certainly awaits, not heeding my warning. You never read to the end of the script, not heeding my warning. Of all the travelers I have led—"

Chloe stared at him. "What did you just say? About the script!"

Scout opened his mouth, and then let it shut. He shook his head. "We'll go, but let it be known I had nothing to do with this. Lead on."

"You're going to tell me how you know about the script." Chloe grabbed Scout and yanked — dodging, ducking, but always moving forward. After minutes of painful pinching from all sides, they reached the rail and Chloe poked her head over the edge.

"Ow!"

"No." Scout released her hair, which he'd practically yanked from her scalp. "Don't look. If you wish me to follow you into this madness, you must promise not to look. When I say leap, jump the railing. You will fall, but not far. I'll be right behind."

Chloe rolled her eyes. "Fine. You like to be in charge, don't you?"

"One. Two." Scout peeked over the edge as they walked forward slowly. "Last step. Right here! Ignore what you see, and jump!"

Chloe had leaped fences many times at home. It was an easy enough maneuver, made easier because she could see through to her landing. This was altogether different. Chloe flung her legs and body over the top rail, glanced down and, like a frightened cat, clawed for the lower crossbar. She caught it and hung, her dangling feet fighting to find footing back on the road.

Hundreds of feet below, huge rocks jutted upward as water crashed in angry white foam against them.

"Scout!" she screamed. "Pull me — "

He peeped over the fence, grunted, and smashed her whitening fingers with his own.

"Aaahh!" Chloe fell. For two seconds. Her feet struck water and she plunged beneath, surfacing quickly. There were no rocks, only a peaceful river, and ten feet above her was the bridge.

Ignore what you see.

She drifted away from the bridge. *Come on. You said you would —*

For a moment, Scout's limp leg appeared over the rail, but the drift of people knocked him to the ground. Above, a dragon shrieked and dived down toward the bridge.

"Scout!" Chloe screamed. "The sky!"

Then he came all at once, rolling over the edge, breaking free of arms and legs and landing on his side in what must have been a painful splash. His head popped up. The dragon circled not two feet above him. It snarled and searched the width of the river.

Scout winked at Chloe and dived — she watched anxiously as Scout's shape tracked the dragon beneath the waterline, each stroke labored but quick. Then, with a tremendous splash, Scout burst up, knife raised, and plunged it into the dragon's belly.

The dragon recoiled as Scout and drops of black blood crashed down together into the river. The beast clawed at his stomach, screeched, and vanished from sight.

"It's not often that you get such a chance against one of Pindle's children. How I hope it was the same one with whom I shared a nest! You can believe that a wound from that blade will sicken her for days to come."

"She couldn't see us?" Chloe called.

"Vaepor's illusion is so great his own Senseri can't see through it anymore. She saw the gorge, the rocks — "

"But I sees you jest fine, lad." A strong hand grabbed for Scout's collar and hauled him onto a flat raft of logs.

Chloe breathed deep and dived. It was instinct, but one that made little sense. The water was clear and cool and shallow. There would be no place to hide below.

Above, she saw the bottom of the raft. She couldn't leave Scout. Yet something below the waterline felt comfortable, safe. Like home. Inside, she felt a twinge of longing.

It was her father who first taught her to swim. Her father who brought her to the Melmanie pool for practice. It all changed with the accident, of course, but even now he would be proud of how strong a swimmer she'd become.

Chloe kicked hard and glided beneath the logs. Her air supply was running low—

Glurp. An arm rounded her waist, hauled her upward, and pitched her onto the raft. Scout grabbed Chloe under her arms and pulled her away from the edge.

Scout hung his head. "I thought you'd drowned." His legs buckled and he sat with a plop.

A squat fellow with giant forearms leaped out of the water and landed feetfirst on the raft. It was a strange sight, and despite her exhaustion, Chloe started to giggle.

"Well, I never known a human to stay near two minutes under water. You be part fish."

"No." Chloe breathed deep. "But what are you?"

"River dwarf," he and Scout both said, though Scout spoke through a scowl.

"And what have I done, other than rescue a cripple from certain death, that you would frown at who I am? I am Tuftunder, from the proud line of Tunders — "

"Proud line?" Scout repeated. "Thieves."

"Borrowers."

"Liars."

"A creative lot. And who be you to speak? The river pirate's life never lacks for adventure, and" — he winked and fixed his gaze on Chloe's scar — "we even remember it."

"And what makes you think I don — "

"I agree, wise dwarf." Scout kicked her foot. "We were on the Pilgrimage."

"And fell off the bridge? 'Tis the first time in my two hundred years that I've seen such a thing," Tuftunder said. "Lucky you are that my mood was generous and my fortunes favorable." He walked over to a chest and opened it. *Mountain stone!* Chloe stared at the treasure, and Tuftunder slammed the lid. "Foolish elves."

"How did you get those?" Chloe asked.

Tuftunder picked up his pole and rafted them faster down river. "You wouldn't be rememberin', so there be no harm in bragging a bit. See, lass, the

Green River stretches deep into the Unknown Forest, a place you would not dare go."

Chloe bit her tongue.

"Go on, noble dwarf." Scout leaned in. "Tell of your exploits."

He smiled broadly. "If you insist."

Tuftunder's chest swelled as he began his tale. "Elves, especially wood elves, are a dumb collection — filled with fear they are. I floated a silent raft into the Unknown and hollered, 'Vaepor be I. Give up your stones.' Mountain stones dropped like apples from the trees. Mind you, Tuftunder is the only river dwarf with courage to float into that accursed forest." He stroked the wooden chest. "But the reward 'tis grand."

"You pretended to be that beastly thing?" Chloe scooted backward on the raft.

"Beastly? Perhaps to some. But Vaepor pays a pretty penny for these stones." Tuftunder paused and lowered his voice. "Lately, he pays a pretty penny for children — perhaps not lame ones, but strange, pretty ones. 'Keep your eyes open,' he's been saying of late."

Pretty. He called me pretty. Chloe straightened, and the thought washed over her.

He also wants to sell you to Vaepor.

The second thought was new; an unknown voice pushed into her brain. Chloe turned toward Scout, who peered off into the distance. It wasn't his voice she'd heard. At least she didn't think it was.

"Don't take us to It," Chloe said.

"Now you have a problem with that? Ease, lassie. Enjoy the ride. You were walkin' Its way on your own, why shouldn't I benefit from the deal?"

Night soon felt thick and heavy, and the river sounded wider, stronger. Wilder.

"Soon the river will fork and we will veer right, toward Wayward Mountain." Scout spoke, his voice monotone. "The river will tumble down, beneath that peak. There, Tuftunder will try to remove us. We must not get off the raft. No matter what, we stay together on this raft until we pop out the other side."

"Out the other side are the Safelands," Chloe said. "I know that like I know my name. And the river flows into the bay. It's a beautiful bay."

"It's a horrifying bay. Who filled your mind with these tales?"

"That doesn't matter." Chloe peeked at Tuf-tunder, who was poling without any attention to his passengers. "What's under the mountain, Scout?"

"No," he said.

"What do you mean, no?"

"Simple word, really. It means that at this time it might be best for you *not* to be thinking about what's ahead."

Chloe crossed her arms, stared at Scout, and exploded. "Had you jumped sooner, we would not be here. You're the reason I'm floating at night with a nasty, smelly dwarf!"

"Hardly smelly," muttered Tuftunder.

"If you know so much, fearless guide, don't you think it's time you tell me where I'm going?"

Scout sat back and spoke quietly. "Under Way-ward Mountain lies what you want most, Chloe. It's how the dwarfs will lure you."

"There." She stretched and lay back down. "Was that so hard? Doesn't sound so bad. What I want most ... My mom and a big steak and Grandpa's hug and to wake up in Aldo's — "

"Quit your yammering!" Tuftunder hissed. "We're being followed."

Chloe glanced back. She couldn't see more than ten feet in the mist. Tuftunder reached his hand into the water. "Three hundred yards, I'd say. Likely comin' after what I've rightfully stolen."

And then Scout did perhaps the bravest of all things.

He stood and lunged at the chest of stones, and shoved the entire crate into the water.

"Think, Chloe!" Scout yelled. "Remember home."

"You fool!" Tuftunder raised his pole above Scout's head.

For a moment, her mind blanked, and then a face rushed in. *Dad? Will you please look at me?*

In the water, stones floated to the surface, burning a brilliant blue and leaving a breadcrumb trail behind them.

"My stones!" The dwarf brought the pole down on Scout's bad leg and dived into the water. Scout cried out as the dwarf swam furiously from stone to stone, stuffing them into his pockets.

Scout reached for the pole and staggered to his knees. He pushed the raft forward with a groan. "Now, Chloe. Think of me."

"What?" She shook her head and focused on Scout's twisted leg. Floating stones turned gray and then disappeared into the night. From a great distance back, Tuftunder screamed, "Me stones. Me raft, me — Help!"

Scout stared at Chloe. "There is something back there. Can you" — he winced and reached Chloe the pole — "take a shift?"

She nodded and clasped the grip. She'd not used a raft pole before and was not certain how to hold it correctly even now, but she sank the rod deep into the mud and pushed until her shoulders ached.

Hours passed and dawn broke, and still they urged on their now-drifting raft. The river had indeed widened, so much so that it more resembled a lake, but always the pole struck bottom.

The swift current that had carried them so far now meandered about. At times the raft swirled aimlessly, with neither Chloe nor Scout owning the strength to stop its spin. Other times, the logs caught a quick drift and forged ahead, sending Chloe sprawling onto her belly.

"I've never been on a river like this," she said. "At home the Snake River winds, but it never throws you down."

Scout stretched, staggered to his feet, and reached for the pole. Chloe collapsed with a groan.

"There's much beneath our feet to change the water's direction." Scout squinted over his shoulder. "I can't see anyone behind us. Perhaps he exercised his revenge on the dwarf and that was that."

Chloe nodded and watched Scout battle the current.

"Scout?" she asked softly. He didn't answer. "Scout? I lost it with you back there, and I'm sorry. I'm afraid I'm not very good at adventures. I'm the boring one in our family."

Scout laughed. It was rare to hear the sound, and it rang so clear and free that she laughed too.

"Boring?" Scout asked. "I doubt — "

"What is that?" Chloe interrupted, pointing in front of the raft. Water rose like a small wall, churning and foaming and drawing them near.

"That is the squeeze. All this water crowds through that channel, and then the river speeds and twists and the rapids overtake it. We shoot beneath the bridge spanning the Northern Road and from there on it's a wild ride to the roots of Wayward Mountain."

"Rapids. On this raft?" They pitched to the left and bobbed beneath the water. Chloe slipped her fingers in the cracks between the logs. "It won't — "

"Stay together." Scout poled. "No, it won't. The banks are foul — we can't land. Our friend Tuftunder would have brought us certain doom. Without him, we may just have delayed ..."

Chloe nodded. He didn't need to finish. Her plan had failed.

They reached the channel. On the near side swirled a cauldron that sucked water from the larger river, churned it into white froth, and then whisked it into the rapid-filled smaller river ahead.

Scout grabbed her hand. "Lay down and grab the edge. Don't let go."

"Of the raft, or you?" she yelled as they spun nearer to the gap.

"Both." Scout grimaced, and in they flew.

The front lip of the raft dipped beneath the waterline and the raft followed. They sank, struck an underwater tow, and popped out again. Chloe gasped for air and lifted her head off the beams. Ahead was the Northern Bridge.

"It would be strange if there were people waiting for us, right?"

"Waiting? Nobody's waiting."

"So," Chloe continued, "if I did see someone on the bridge—"

"You won't." Scout said. "The Pilgrimage—" Scout looked ahead and quickly glanced back to her. "We can't be seen, not here. Get beneath the raft!"

He released her hand and rolled into the froth. Chloe did the same. Only their fingertips would be visible from above, and they should be easily missed in the waves and white caps.

Thud.

The raft jerked down into the water and struck Chloe's head, but she felt little. Instead, her body went limp and she closed her eyes.

CHLOE CAME TO with a splitting headache. Far above her, unnamed stars twinkled, larger and closer than those in her own nighttime sky, and around her stretched mountains, deep and ominous. Their shadows rose up and ate the stars on either side.

She pitched and bobbed and moaned, and Scout hurried to her. "Welcome back, Chloe."

"The sneaky little fish chooses to wake. How pleasant for us all," Tuftunder spat. "Were I commandeering this raft, which I'm not, I'd be making you swim behind." He wriggled and collapsed onto his back. Chloe blinked. Tuftunder was tied — hand, foot, and chest — with thick rope.

"What happened?" she asked.

"I'll leave that explanation to my brother." Scout leaned back on his elbows.

"You have a brother?"

"He does."

Nob waved and poled forward. The raft skipped over a wave and landed smoothly on the other side. He gave a bashful smile. "I am a ferryman, you know."

Chloe's jaw dropped and she propped herself up, then raised a finger.

"How could you ... and Scout ... and that dwarf ..."

Nob grinned. "I've been following you for some time, not knowing who was in front of me. I was curious, though, as nobody falls off the bridge, especially to sail down this river. When I caught the scent of dragon blood, I prepared for the worst, but it was this dwarf who floated my way, and I scooped him up. Fortunately for me, he's far from mute."

"Mute you say? *Mutiny*, I say. That's what we should be starting, lassy. From what I gather, this Nob left you in the cold, isn't that right?"

Chloe said nothing. *He is right.*

Nob breathed deeply. "The dwarf has me there, and you aren't the first one I've let down either. Fear got the best of me, but I didn't leave you alone. I knew my brother would take better care of you than I ever could … He always does." He hung his head.

"Go on." Chloe stood and put her hand on his shoulder. "You're here now."

Nob lifted his gaze. "So when the river widened, I passed you in the fog and dragged the mouthy dwarf onto the bridge. I threw him onto your raft, neither knowing his weight nor that your head was inches beneath. I'm so sorry."

Chloe hugged Nob from behind. "I am so glad you're here. Will you stay?"

He nodded.

"Oh, how touching." Tuftunder struggled against the rope and rolled onto his side with a huff. "Enjoy each other's company. Soon you'll be in waters only I know."

Chloe ignored the dwarf and stared at Scout and Nob. *Brothers!* She didn't need to ask their story. Scout was the leader, confident like Grif, only kinder. Nob was Q. Much quieter when Scout was around.

Gradually, Chloe's sea legs returned, and she plunked down behind Nob. "Thanks again for coming for me," she whispered.

"You don't need me." He didn't turn.

"Secholit seems to think I do."

Nob puffed out a long blast of air. "Yes, lady. So I came back. But I'm not a very ..."

"What?"

The raft pitched downward and all went black.

"Nob!" Scout said. "Did we go in the tunnel? Are we heading toward Wayward Mountain?"

Nob poled hard. "I've never felt waters like these before."

"And won't likely again." The dwarf chuckled.

"Remember, Chloe," Scout shouted. "Remember anything!"

"Oh, right!" *Pancakes*. Her stomach growled. The thought slid easily into her mind. *Mom's buttermilk pancakes*.

Her stone glowed blue and lit up the tunnel through which they hurtled.

Scout jumped over to Tuftunder and shook him. "Where does this end?"

"In her lair. Your oh-so-gifted Nob lefted when he should have twice righted. Now we're all as good as dead."

Scout nodded. "Did we pass two rights, Nob?"

"We passed ten. How was I to know?" He rubbed his face. "I should have known. I shouldn't have come."

They swirled deeper, bouncing off rock and rock wall, desperate to stay on the raft.

"What's in the lair?" Chloe shouted. "It can't be as bad as all that."

Scout peeked over at Nob.

Tuftunder winked. "She's worse."

And with that, the raft accelerated toward whatever danger awaited them.

Chloe loved water rides. Partly for the whoosh, but more for the splash.

There was no splash.

It was just down and down and down. Chloe couldn't believe a mountain's roots could reach so deep. But eventually the raft slowed and drifted into a still pool. There was still not a shred of natural light, and no matter how hard she remembered, a dull gray glint was all that came from her stone.

"Swim to the shore," Tuftunder grunted. "And quick. Before she sucks us in."

"Do not leave this raft." Scout reached for Nob's arm.

"He's a fool," Tuftunder snorted.

"He's a dwarf," shouted Scout.

Nob's breath was heavy. "Lady, this is your quest. What do you want me to do?"

Chloe held up her stone and searched the dull shoreline. "We need to reach the bay; that's my goal. But I can't stand this water anymore." She looked over at Scout. "You said I'd see what I wanted, and I guess I do. I want to land." She exhaled. "Nob?"

Scout buried his head in his hands. "That was not beneath this mountain. We're off course."

Chloe closed her eyes and fought to remember her maps. "No, this is right. It's where we need to be. We can walk out to the Safelands. I wrote a way out."

"A wise decision, lassy," Tuftunder whispered. "Though a wee bit ill informed. Now will someone release me? I will need my legs if you get my meanin'."

Scout groped toward Tuftunder, and with three quick slashes set the dwarf free. Nob stretched his pole toward shore, and the raft slid silently into sand.

"May I suggest you attempt a faster exit from this place?" Tuftunder leaped ashore and was gone.

Chloe squinted at the grayish beach. A weight descended on her heart — there was something evil about this darkness. Still, she stepped onto solid ground. Scout and Nob followed. She couldn't bear to look into Scout's eyes. It wasn't the first time she'd ignored his council.

"Help me secure the raft," Nob murmured. "We may need it later." Nob and Scout and Chloe splashed into the water and groaned the raft onto shore.

"Whose lair are we in?" Chloe asked.

Scout shook his head. "I had thought perhaps

fortune had swept us to the meeting place. We're many years too late, but … the lair, this I've always taken as myth. Nob?"

Nob squinted. "I see no danger, but my spirit feels one. Tuftunder ran that way."

"Then let's go the other," Chloe said.

They traipsed along the waterline. Chloe had felt many emotions since her arrival, but the despair of that place was overwhelming. Every thought was filled with hate; every step took her deeper into disgust. They'd marched an hour, and still the drab scenery had not changed.

"This was your route, Chloe," Scout hissed. "This was your decision. We could be in a wide place, but instead we are here, in this hideous, cavernous — "

He suddenly grabbed Chloe's arm, and Nob grasped Scout's. They looked at each other's hands, and then up at each other's rage-filled faces. Slowly, they released their grips.

"I don't like my thoughts here. Angry thoughts, but familiar thoughts. May I suggest that the raft is our only way out?" Scout said. "This river flows in. It must exit."

Chloe's jaw tightened at the thought of more water, but she knew he was right. This shore was changing them.

"Fine!" She kicked at the sand. "Back to the raft. There's nothing down here I want."

Darkness gobbled up all sense of time, and in the forever space of their return shuffle, Chloe felt hope drain out of her. She forced her mind back home, but even there she found no joy.

Her family—who cares if she saw them again? She'd leave Nob and Scout if she could.

"We should have reached it by now." Nob searched the area. Another five minutes passed.

"It's gone," Scout said, then pitched forward. "Well, most of it." Beneath his feet, the pole lay in the sand.

Chloe fell onto her knees. "I couldn't take it. It was me. I messed up."

Scout said nothing.

Nob plopped beside her. "We're still together. It could be worse ... Scout, do you feel that?"

He nodded. "A cool breeze. Something comes."

Chloe jumped to her feet, and Nob reached for the pole.

"Who goes there?" Scout yelled. "We demand safe passage through."

The breeze grew stronger, circled them, and drew them forward.

"Give me your hands!" Nob grabbed Scout's and

Chloe's, and they flew forward, squinting and blinking, toward a pinpoint light.

Chloe cracked an eyelid as her body swirled helplessly and her feet lifted off the ground. Above them — hundreds of feet, thousands of feet — she could see an opening and the clear blue of the sky.

"Ooh!" The foot of a dwarf kicked her head as he spun by. She ducked as a wood elf skimmed her scalp.

"Wind funnel!" Scout screamed.

Chloe squeezed Nob's hand. "We're trapped inside the mountain! This is not how I wrote it! Nothing is like I thought it would be!"

They were not swirling alone. Thousands of creatures, from fleet-footed cheetahs and tumbling snapping turtles, to trolls and gnomes and elves and men and winged giants with their hands on sword hilts, all spun limp and lifeless.

The air about her was so thick with creatures that Chloe caught just a moment's glimpse of the shaft's walls. This wasn't a thin hole that reached down from above. This was an entire hollowed-out mountain.

A tiny dragon thunked Nob square in the chest. He gasped and Chloe broke free from his grasp.

"Scout?" Chloe yelled as her body whizzed by his.

"These are Old Retinyans!" he called. "I don't know if they are living or dead."

"Dazed." The voice echoed from below, and Chloe twisted to catch a glimpse of a woman, hooded in white, standing on a rock and unaffected by the whirling winds.

"Scout, it can't be!" Nob said.

"Poor, frightened ferryman. A bit late to the meeting, wouldn't you say? Is that how you greet royalty?" she said, calmly raising her hand. Nob's body crashed against the rocky wall and kept spinning.

"Younger sister, is this how you greet your royal brothers?" Scout shouted. "I am Biln. This is Nob. We wandered this land together."

That's your sister?

"That was a different life, *Scout*. When all was set right. When this lair was not my prison. Before Secholit fled — "

"I didn't flee."

A shadow darkened the inside of the mountain. "I don't flee." The voice was closer now. "I won't flee."

The wind funnel spun even faster, and then the winds stopped. The host of creatures fell, landing hard on top of the stone slab. Chloe was fortunate. After landing feetfirst on top of a giant's back, she leaped toward a wall as the sky rained man and beast, freed from their merciless spin.

Chloe witnessed far more painful descents. The

shadow that darkened the sky vanished, and in the light she clearly saw four upright figures. Chloe drew nearer. Scout and Blind Secholit stood together. Nob cowered behind Scout. The hooded woman backed away.

"You abandoned me here," she hissed.

"You left me. I never left you." Blind Secholit stepped forward and pointed upward with his staff. "That opening above you was a gift. You've always been free to leave this place."

"Vaepor's funnel cloud was too strong." Her voice cracked. "It held us all in."

"Your courage fell." Another step. "Your anger grew." And another. "I gave you these men and creatures to lead, and you allowed their capture."

Secholit leaned over to a wood elf. He whispered and it opened its eyes.

Then he turned to Chloe. "Did Scout not tell you to stay on the raft?"

She nodded. "But he said that beneath the mountain I'd find what I most wanted."

"Have you?"

"I guess this is the wrong mountain, and I didn't find home. But I did find ... you."

Secholit smiled, but only for a moment. "Your trip will now be more difficult. I see heartache ahead for you, Chloe." He turned to Scout. "But still you are not too late. Nick is near. And as for you, Zophira, you will accompany Chloe and your brothers."

The woman pointed at Chloe. "But she is weak. Isn't there another task?"

Secholit nodded. "Only one, and that is mine to complete." He glanced around the mountain. "Zophira, all these I gave you to lead, I now remove from your command."

Her jaw dropped. "But, sir, only a gifted one can command their respect."

"Agreed." Secholit leaned hard on his walking stick and approached Scout. "Move."

Scout stood aside. Nob stared up with wide eyes and gradually straightened.

"Yes." Secholit tapped him on the head with his staff. "You will do well. I place this army under your command."

"I don't … I haven't … Maybe Scout would be a better choice," Nob stammered.

"A snow toad would be a better choice," Zophira muttered. "You can't do this to me!"

Blind Secholit turned toward her slowly, his face stern. "Where have you come from, Zophira?" And Secholit grew, not in inches or in feet. He swept Zophira up in his hand and grew until his head shielded the sky. Chloe rubbed her eyes, blinked, and when she looked next, Secholit was back to normal size and reaching for his stick, while Zophira sat pouting in the corner.

"Did you just, uh, get really big?" Chloe asked.

If Secholit heard her, he gave no sign. "Vaepor's winds seek to return. Nob, you will know when Retinya needs you, but for now, remain with Chloe. There is an order in everything. I will stay and wake the others, but I will send two more with you." Secholit hobbled toward the dragon that had collided with Nob. "Pindle, wake." The tiny dragon opened one eye, then another, and offered a large yawn. Pindle was a perfect miniature of Flit, but in Chloe size.

"How cute." Chloe took a step forward and stopped. "And old." His leathery face wrinkled beyond deep.

"Good morning, Pindle," Secholit said. "Your children need you. All but Flit have turned and now roam Retinya."

"Which?" Pindle looked around. "Oh my." He bowed to Scout and Nob and the woman, and lastly to Secholit. "How have I come here?"

"You came to the Last Gathering of Old Retinya. During the war council, Vaepor spun the winds and trapped you in the mountain. It was not to have happened." Secholit glanced down, and Zophira looked away quickly.

"Vaepor," Pindle hissed. "How I hate that misty beast."

"Then may I introduce you to Chloe." Secholit smiled. "She now holds Retinya's future in her hands."

Pindle hopped toward her and set his wings in her palms. "Then you will hold mine."

Secholit turned toward a sleeping figure slumped against the wall. "Finally, Groundspeaker, the soil needs you."

A slim man blinked and rose, and fell to his knees.

"The ground has become foul. Make it new." Secholit faced the group. "All of you. Chloe must pass through the Safelands to the bay and then reach Shadowton. This was her plan, made without consultation." Secholit sighed. "Though the consequences are great, it's the road she must now travel. From there she will rejoin the Pilgrimage and enter the City of Reckoning and finally reach the pool." He paused. "To complete the task I have given her, this must happen." He turned to Chloe. "From there, she alone knows what to do."

"And now, farewell, friends."

"Wait!" Chloe ran up to Secholit. "I don't want

you to get big on me, but I still think you could do this whole deal better than me. I mean, especially ..." She scanned the cave and lowered her voice. "The last part of my job. I mean, I lose my temper and I lost Nick, and I usually mess up."

Secholit folded his arms. "Perfect."

A giant updraft swept them into the air, lifting them higher and higher toward the freedom of blue sky. They popped out the top of the mountain and landed with a thud in the cool snow of its peak.

For a minute, nobody spoke.

"That was where Old Retinya took our last stand." Pindle shook his head. "Inside the Hollow Mount we met for one last council of war, but the ground spread word to Vaepor, and we've been trapped ever since."

"But you're out now, right?" Chloe shivered.

"Yes, Chloe. We are out."

Nob took a few steps and slipped to his knees. "I just wish I still had my raft."

From behind, a blast of air whooshed out of the mountain. Chloe looked up and watched as a speck whistled down, growing larger and squarer, until *poof*!

The raft landed flat in the snow beside Scout.

"Well, now." Nob grinned. "That's something you don't see every day."

WIND WHIPPED AROUND THE PEAK, wrapping Chloe's shins and knees with layers of white. Her clothes — still damp from her river ride — plunged freezing needles into her legs. She knew she wouldn't last long.

"This is what he does." Zophira drew herself up. "He rescues from one danger only to throw us into another. Give me the comfort of the mountain!"

"Comfort?" Pindle said. "Let it go. Think now. I could carry a few of you down, but would not have the strength to ascend again."

"At least we have some firewood. There's not much use for a raft up here." Scout dusted himself off.

A grin spread across Chloe's face. "But there is for a sled!" She jumped aboard.

Nob's face lit up. "If I had my pole I could steer —
I knew I shouldn't have left that in the mountain. As
it is we'd end up smashed — "

Shuff!

His pole stabbed the peak and quivered like
an arrow. Nob puzzled at the sky a moment, then
grabbed the wood and muscled it out of the snow.
He shoved Chloe and the raft a few yards forward.

"Everyone on the mountain ferry."

Scout and Groundspeaker joined them. They all
turned toward Zophira.

"No," she said. "There is no chance."

Nob gazed downward. "We could use a little tail-
wind, that's all."

"Then you, my young general brother, will need
to produce it yourself."

"You know I can't." Nob swallowed hard.

"Of course you can't. That gift wasn't given you.
You were given a water rat's gift."

"Stop." Scout strode toward the woman. "Younger
sister Zophira, stop. There's no need to beat down on
Nob."

"Oh, isn't there?" She stiffened. "Why weren't
you two trapped at council? Wasn't it the cowardice
of Nob? Did he not purposely keep you from reaching the meeting? Or did his knowledge of the rivers

suddenly vanish?" She pointed at Nob. "Nothing but a plot to steal my position."

"That was long ago!" Scout's voice strengthened. "Would it have served Retinya well if all three of us had been trapped? You refused Blind Secholit's rescue. Would you have taken an offer from us?"

"Yes! But is this a rescue? Forced company with a coward, a know-it-all" — she stared at Chloe — "and a useless child who clearly has forgotten everything she once knew."

Chloe's hand shot up and rubbed her scar.

"And by the way, how is that leg treating you? Has the limp remained?"

"Silence!" shouted the dragon.

Throughout the argument, Chloe'd been watching Pindle, who'd kept his head buried in his wings. But now he fluttered up and landed on Chloe's shoulders. "I rest on the only wise one among you. Stop it, children ... noble children, but children nonetheless. We have only one pursuit, and whatever your family history may be, choose now to lay it aside."

Nob peeked up, but nobody else moved.

"Zophira, are you not able to summon the winds? But you were too weak to escape the mountain." She raised her hand to speak, but then let her mouth fall shut.

"Nob, a great seaman, but fearful when you should be brave. And Scout, a leader on land, but prone to self-importance. Remember whose you are. Remember the glory of Old Retinya when you walked a peaceful land. Decide to end this petty squabble."

"And get on the raft, before Chloe freezes."

The last words were so low, they rumbled the mountain.

"He speaks again." Scout smiled.

"What was that?" Chloe asked.

"Groundspeaker." The name thundered again. "For too long this ground has been subject to the enemy." The thin man bent over, his lips inches from the snow. "It's time to reclaim THIS GROUND."

The mountain shook and Zophira leaped onto Scout. The snow lurched beneath their feet and a crack formed around them.

"Avalanche!" Nob grabbed the pole. "We need wind, sister!"

Zophira raised her arm and a strong gust hurtled the raft forward, down the mountain. Chloe looked over her shoulder. The snowcap had broken loose and thundered down behind them.

"Can you go faster?" Chloe cried.

Nob dug in his pole and the sled banked sharply

to the left. To Chloe, it felt like surfing — they lifted and surged forward while showers of snow curled over their heads.

The sled popped out of the wave of snow, placing them clear of tumbling snow.

"Well done, Nob," Chloe said. "You're a genius — "

He pointed at a range of jagged rocks jutting out in front of them. "Now the work begins." Nob rolled up a sleeve.

Scout grabbed Chloe from behind, and the small group huddled together on the sled's middle while Nob stood braced on one side.

Zophira whispered, "I did not want to die."

Scout leaned into her. "Watch your brother."

"Yah!" Nob leaped from one edge of the raft to the other, correcting and micro-correcting their path. The sled zipped left and right. Rock formations blurred by with dizzying speed.

Chloe's fingers dug into Scout's arm, but he paid no attention. Ten minutes. Twenty minutes. An hour, and still the sled skipped.

Finally, they slowed. A wash of spray hit Chloe's face.

Melting snow!

As the sled struck a slushy patch, they all tumbled forward and crunched to a halt not one yard from a rocky outcrop twenty feet tall and three times as wide. Nob lifted his pole and with it his gaze. There would have been no way around this boulder.

Chloe's hands released Scout. Nob turned, dropped his pole, and collapsed into the slush. Zophira was first to his side.

"Brave Nob. My brave brother." She stroked his head. "Quickly, a covering; his body shakes."

Groundspeaker offered his, and soon Scout located a dry nook in the rock.

"It will be a cold, wet night. But look!" He pointed down into the valley. "The Green River. There it is. And to the left, Chloe? That desert means we are nearer. The Safelands."

"The Safelands," Zophira whispered.

"The Safelands." Pindle flapped his wings.

"The Safelands," Groundspeaker rumbled, and the rock shook.

"But are they still safe?" Nob whispered and blinked.

Nobody answered, and Chloe fell into an uneasy sleep.

● ● ●

Chloe woke up shivering. There would be no falling back to sleep, she knew, and so she quickly rose.

Scout, Nob, and Zophira huddled in cloaks laid out on the raft, but Groundspeaker and Pindle had gone. She scrambled up to the top of the rock and peered into the valley, which had been pure darkness the night before.

"Beautiful."

"Isn't it?"

Chloe startled and knelt down. "Qujan? You found me!" She hugged the Quint, and felt warmth fill her body.

"Moving between worlds provides no difficulty for a Quint. Convincing Quill that such a move is necessary—this is a challenge. Listen, Chloe, Nick's book is no longer black. It is gray. This is both good and concerning. It means some life yet remains, but for whatever reason—Quill cannot see—Vaepor suddenly has no need of Nick, no want of him. I do not expect he will survive unless you find him."

"I'm doing my best, but everyone tells me different things! Secholit said I'd need him, but now it's all, 'Get to the pool.' To Scout, Nick is always first. You told me to forget him, now I'm supposed to find him?"

"I know." Qujan reached over and stroked Chloe's hair. "Life changes. Horrible things happen." Qujan then cupped Chloe's chin. "And then plans change.

To be sure, you must reach the pool, but I feel you may find your friend on the way." She hugged Chloe again. "You don't know how long I've desired to do this."

Qujan breathed deeply as she broke the embrace and together she and Chloe stared at the landscape before them. The northern run of the Green River snaked on like a thin ribbon through a sea of brown. Along its banks, trees and bushes grew, creating twenty feet of life on either side. Directly below, in that thin stretch of green, a deer — no, two — bounded through the brush. To the left of the river, all was sand, unending sand.

There, nothing moved.

Well, almost nothing.

A lone figure walked the desert, tracking away from the base of the mountain on which Chloe stood. A giant vulture circled around its head.

"Why would anyone walk there?" Chloe asked.

"Because that is where he needs to walk." Zophira climbed up beside her. "He goes where the ground is foul. He goes to speak against Vaepor, and to turn the ground back to our side."

Chloe rose and faced Zophira. She didn't return the glance.

"That's Groundspeaker?"

She nodded.

"But doesn't he see the vulture?" Chloe pointed at the circling bird.

Zophira laughed. "Oh, I doubt Pindle will devour him. Unless, of course, Groundspeaker insults his family."

"But I thought—"

"They would travel with us? They must prepare our path. Without Groundspeaker, the dirt beneath your feet would send word and give us away. Not even Scout could find us safe passage."

Chloe slowly lowered herself onto the rock and whispered to Qujan, "Why isn't she talking to you?"

Qujan glanced at Zophira. "She cannot see me, or hear me—but she does sense me. I'm sure of this."

"What did you say?" asked Zophira.

Chloe smiled quickly in Zophira's direction and ducked her head lower. "Then why can I?"

"That is a question for Salvador." Qujan smiled. "I could reveal. I could become visible, but then I could not return to the hall. I would forever live above ground."

Zophira frowned. "Who do you speak to?"

"Sorry," Chloe said. "Active imagination."

"Put well," whispered Qujan.

"I do not understand what makes you valuable,

far more so than any girl I've met. Why would Blind Secholit gather three rulers of old to see *you* on your way?" Zophira stared down at her. "What are you to do?"

"Say nothing," said Qujan.

"Well, he told me to keep what I heard to myself."

"Who did?"

"Secholit … and Nob."

"Nob." Zophira laughed. "You still trust him. Don't you see his fear?"

Chloe stood up. "No."

Qujan bumped Chloe. "Get out of this conversation, it will not end well. Quickly, ask her how her seven sisters are getting on. Especially Kyrie."

"Zophira …" Chloe looked back at the Quint before she continued. "How's your family doing? Your sisters, all seven of them. I'd especially like to hear about Kyrie."

Zophira's face whitened and she staggered backward.

"Nobody apart from Secholit himself knows her sisters' names." Qujan's face was stern. "Zophira's not really Retinyan, though she plays the part. Your knowledge of Kyrie shows her you have power."

"Good morning." Scout popped up between them, and Zophira bristled. "I didn't know you two were up." He glanced at Chloe and frowned. "Is everything all right?"

"Fine, brother. As the … as the … only females in this strange grouping, we were getting better acquainted." Zophira turned toward Chloe and slowly approached. She hugged her loosely, and Chloe felt her tremble. "I thank you for taking me into your confidence. You can be assured that your secrets are safe with me." She released Chloe and climbed down the rock.

"Your siblings' secrets are safe with me as well," Chloe called, freezing Zophira, who quickly sprung down off the rock.

Scout tongued the inside of his cheek. "I've not seen her shaken like that before. What did you tell her?"

"Nothing. I have no idea what —"

"There are … things I could tell you about my dear sister." Scout turned away. "She's not the safest location to deposit hidden thoughts."

"Hey." Chloe tugged at his shirt, but he did not move. "Any teenager could see she just said that to get at you. I didn't tell her a thing, I promise. Are you angry at me?"

Scout slumped, glanced over his shoulder, and closed his eyes. "I don't know what I am. She and I —"

"Are like royalty. Hello! What's that about? There's a little secret you've kept from me, right?"

He nodded and stared down into the valley. "Another time. Did you see Groundspeaker's path? We'll want to follow it. Before the winds" — he peeked in the direction Zophira had gone — "from whatever source, blow away any trace."

Scout followed his sister, leaving Chloe and Qujan alone.

"Please, Qujan, come with us. Just for a while. I won't talk to you in front of anybody." Chloe grabbed onto her arm. "I'm stuck in a world I thought I would know, but it's all different."

"I need to return before Quill wakes and finds me gone, but I need to make one thing clear. You feel you wrote this world. This is not true. The ideas and pictures you put down were given to you. You and Nick sorted through this glimpse. When you were working on your script, you each threw away the unpleasant and focused on what you felt were the most desirable parts of the land. So although you worked together, you wrote two very different worlds."

"I don't get it."

"You struggle here because your heart is still in the past, in a time before your scar, when your family held you near. It's where you live, where you long to be.

"Because you live looking back, the glimpse you wrote is also in the past — the Retinya of old, where there was joy, where there were happy endings — but your invisible elven kingdoms, the magnificent beautiful cities ... The truth is that place only exists in our memories.

"Nick lives in the near future. He dreams of a time, very soon, when he might be able see in your world again. He dreams of being well. Nick wrote Retinya's near future, and so he moves through this land with ease." Qujan forced a smile.

"But it comes to this: It is time for both of you to live in the present. To finish the task Secholit gave you. Do not run —"

"I know, don't run from my father."

"No. From yourself. For you, my precious one, are beautiful."

Qujan gently kissed Chloe's head and disappeared. *Beautiful.* Chloe touched her face. *Could it be?*

● ● ●

They broke camp and set out, finishing the last section of downward slope in excellent time. To the right, the river bubbled and beckoned, but Scout made straight for the first of Groundspeaker's footprints that led through the desert.

I don't want to be trudging through this waste-land. I want to be near the gentle waves.

Nob bumped Chloe's shoulder with his. "Do you remember, lady, where those waters came from?"

Chloe frowned. "Why does everyone around here know what I'm thinking?"

"You've been staring at the river for a minute, maybe more. That river flowed beneath the mountain," he continued. "Evil, dark thoughts accompany those waters. They have not changed."

She exhaled hard and pushed her hand through matted hair. *Oh, for a bath.*

"Okay." Chloe pried her gaze off the river. "Through the sand."

THE TINY BAND SET OUT slowly across the dunes. It wasn't hot; it wasn't that type of desert. But it was dry. Dry and brown and forever. Despite Nob's warning, Chloe couldn't take her eyes off the river and its bank, where fish jumped and rabbits played.

"What would happen if we left this path?" Chloe asked, her gaze fixed on two squirrels playing tag around a tree.

Nob glanced around his feet. "I don't know anymore. There was a time when we ran across these sands. We lured our enemies here and ..."

"Go on," Zophira called. "Tell her."

Nob shook his head, so Zophira continued. "The Sands would do the rest."

The sand looked like ordinary sand, not that they had much in Minnesota. Chloe bent over and

222

scooped up a handful, and let it sift out between her fingers. As it filtered down, she had to stifle a gasp. "This is Snake River sand. Dad and I used to build huge sandcastles from this stuff back home." She leaned forward to pull an armful nearer. "Of course, you need water." She leaned forward again, stretched too far, and thudded softly on her belly with a laugh.

"Get up, Chloe!" Nob grabbed her leg, but she kicked free.

"There's nothing here to — Oh!"

Sand shifted beneath her and the firm desert floor gave way. Below was nothing but endless dark. Above, lips — giant, sandy lips — closed over her.

"Quick!" a voice called from beneath her. "Digest it. It's been too long."

Burning liquid covered Chloe's ankles.

"Oh, Nob! Scout! Secholit!"

Her mountain stone blazed blue, and with its glow the cavernous stomach heaved, the lips opened, and Chloe shot back into daylight, landing hard on a sandy mound.

Nob bolted toward her, dodging sand mouths that opened and closed on both sides of him.

Scout shouted, "No, Nob! You're off the path!"

"My legs! They're burning!" Chloe threw her arms around Nob's neck.

Nob swept sand over her feet, her calves, and her knees, until soon the burning lessened. "I can't say there may not be a mark, lady."

Chloe closed her eyes. "It's all right. I'm okay. You came for me."

Nob nodded, lifted Chloe, and sped her back to the path, where Scout took her and lay her down.

"Nobody comes back out of the sand. I thought we'd lost you." Scout bent over, his brow furrowed. "And you, Nob. Lead and protect, but don't be foolish, brother. What if you hadn't reached safety?"

Zophira smiled. "Then he would be like you, O great designated protector of Nick. Am I not right?"

Scout's teeth clenched. "He left on his own accord."

"And you did not follow him?"

"I couldn't reach ... He refused to be followed."

Zophira walked on leisurely, following Groundspeaker's trail. She paused, but did not turn. "You failed, Scout." Then, calmly, she continued her walk.

Scout gasped and reached for his stomach. Chloe reached over and squeezed his arm.

"She's just —"

"Correct. This time she is correct." He rubbed his bad leg. "I was to lead him."

Chloe stood and brushed the sand off her legs.

"Grandpa Salvador always says you can't lead a man who won't follow. Guess that goes for kids too. Especially now that Nick can see."

Scout turned toward Chloe slowly. "Yes. Back home, he's blind. It's suddenly so clear." He pulled Chloe forward. "We need to find him."

"But didn't you hear Secholit? I need to reach the pool."

"When you reach the pool, you'll need Nick, not me, at your side. I've heard that unseen creatures lurk there ... Creatures only the blind among us can see. It was the blind of Old Retinya who first sensed them. They alerted us of their presence, described their faces, told us of their forms. The blind of Old Retinya were highly honored."

Chloe thought on that. "But Nick's not blind anymore."

"Isn't he?"

They walked in silence, their padded, mile-after-mile shuffle interrupted only by the Sands' occasional roar. Chloe nudged nearer to Nob.

"In a different time, this desert swallowed entire enemy armies." He gestured across the plain. "The Sands were selective, loyal at heart. They took the invaders. They left us."

Sand shifted beside Chloe, and Nob lifted her

away from the gaping mouth. "Where is your allegiance?" he yelled, and the sand slammed shut.

"Now they take whomever they will. These are no longer the Safelands."

Chloe stared at the tatters of her jeans and red marks on her ankles. She couldn't imagine what the crossing would have been without Groundspeaker.

Nob cocked his head slightly. "Do you taste salt?"

Chloe licked her cracked, bleeding lips, and they stung.

Nobody answered. They didn't need to. On the right, the river they'd traced forked and then forked again. A cool, wet breeze caressed Chloe's face.

"Oh, that feels so — Grass!" Beneath her feet, the shuffle of sand gave way to the crunch of dry grass, then soft grass, then lush green sprigs.

"We've reached the delta," Nob whispered.

They weren't the only ones. Beaten trails became worn paths and finally small streets lined with huts and shops. Stern-faced people lost in their own affairs moved about quickly, without giving the four a second glance.

"Seafarers all, come to trade with Shadowton across the bay," Nob said. "Mostly Calainians." He whispered conspiratorially and nodded toward an approaching group. "Their pale skin has earned them the name Palainians." *Pale* did not approach it. Their skin was nearly white, while their hair and eyes were flame red.

"They came from lands in the west and settled in the delta when Old Retinya vanished. But I think this is as far as they will travel, what with Vaepor ruling the land." He thumped his chest. "We water rats are a superstitious sort."

Nob kept speaking, but Chloe couldn't focus. The smell of cooking fish filled the streets and her nostrils. She hadn't eaten well since her meal with the Quints, and this would more than do.

"Can't we stop for food?" Chloe begged, peering through a restaurant window.

"Not here." Scout called back. "Better to slip through."

"Through to where?"

Nob pointed.

Ahead, on the coast, rose a sprawling city, and beyond the many buildings clear blue water sparkled. Not river water, but open water. The kind Chloe'd never visited before. Dad never took her on those kinds of excursions.

Her mountain stone shone, and Nob stopped. "Where did you meet me?"

"Up there. High above."

The glimmer died.

"It would be better if your stone were not noticed." He raised his eyebrows. "We would be less ... desirable." He glanced at Chloe's confused face and continued. "This town deals in many things — stones, weapons, slaves — "

"Like people slaves?"

The scent of salt sharpened, as did the harsh words on the streets. Sailors cursed and caroused, catcalling in Zophira's direction.

She is beautiful, thought Chloe, who stared straight ahead, tucked closely between Nob and Scout. They wound their way onto a main thoroughfare filled with horses and carts, people, and dwarfs. She felt safer among the masses, and they quickly wove their way down to the docks.

Directly in front of Chloe, strongmen unloaded cargo from huge ships. Elsewhere, crates and barrels and chests stacked high on the wharf, waiting to be carried aboard. Shipmen and dockworkers argued with fishermen bobbing in tiny boats. Chloe smiled at the sight.

"We have a big port in Duluth, not far from my house."

Again, the stone glowed. Zophira spun. "Are you

… Is she going to be doing this the entire journey? Give me the stone. I'll silence it."

"It fell to her." Scout stepped between them. "It is connected to her memories. She will carry it."

A small crowd gathered around them, staring at the blue light.

Scout glanced up from his sister. "Does anybody have a ship? We need a berth to Shadowton."

"Just a small skiff will do," added Nob.

"Aye. I have your ship." A river dwarf pushed to the front. "The price will be one blue mountain stone." He never took his eye off Chloe's pocket, where the now-dull rock rested.

"That is not in the barter." Scout turned. "Though I have something else to offer." He limped up to Zophira and stared. "A year of favorable winds."

At first, there was silence. Then a chuckle that gave way to laughter. "You offer what no boy can possess." The voice belonged to a sailor dressed in gray, who now parted the crowd. "I have a ship. I will not sell it, but I sail to Shadowton in the morning and I have plenty of room."

"Well," Chloe said, "that settles tha—"

Nob slapped his hand over her mouth and leaned over. "Slaver."

"My offer still stands," Scout shouted. "What

would a year of tailwinds be worth to you? Think of it. A quick skip to Shadowton. One less day sailing in the Terror's domain."

Terror?

"Prove you have it to offer!" a lone voice called.

Scout turned again to Zophira, whose eyes narrowed. "I am no circus clown who performs for the bidding of these whistling apes!"

"Then do it for Chloe."

Her jaws tightened.

"For Nob and me."

Nothing.

Two more gray-clad sailors pressed in.

Zophira looked to either side. "I'll do it out of hate for a quest so beneath me."

She raised her hand and then turned her palm to the sky. For a moment, all was still; a strange still as the steady, salty breeze fell calm. Then the winds came. They moaned in from the desert, bearing particles of fine sand. Chloe shielded her eyes and turned her back, eyes stinging.

"A witch! She's turned the wind!" a voice called.

People fell to their knees and bowed. "Who are you that the winds obey?"

"Don't bow!" Scout yelled. "She's only a — "

"Oh, let them fall on their faces." Zophira squinted. "It won't hurt them."

"Don't do this," Nob said.

Zophira frowned and raised her hand higher. The wind howled, blowing everything not tied down toward the open water. Oars and nets and people tumbled down the docks. Scout lost his balance. Nob grabbed Chloe's hand and let the wind have its way.

Within seconds the three crashed into one of two posts at the end of the Great Pier.

"Don't you three need a ship? Isn't this what you wanted?" Zophira yelled. "Go! Take your precious Chloe and leave."

"No." Scout took a limping step into the gale, gaining a few feet before tumbling backward. Nob caught his shoulder, but others weren't so lucky. Hundreds of men, women, and river dwarfs shouted and splashed into the water.

"Friends, here!"

A young Calainian held tightly to the mast of his small skiff. "Take it before we all perish!"

They jumped in and Nob quickly made ready.

"Zophira!" Scout hollered.

Crack! The post to which the boat was tied gave way and they washed out into the bay. Hundreds of unmanned ships joined them in a makeshift flotilla.

An hour later, and many miles from the coast, Zophira's wind had calmed to a gentle breeze. Chloe stared at the endless waves, but didn't feel like speaking.

"Will she come back?" Nob asked, without emotion.

"No," said Scout. "She is too bitter."

Chloe looked down. "Was it me?"

Scout nodded. "She couldn't bear to look on one more important than herself."

"I'm not more anything. I mean, she can control the wind."

"But she can't control her own anger."

Chloe thought of Dad, at how long she'd been angry. *If they only knew.*

23

THE CALAINIAN BOAT pitched and rolled for three days. Chloe passed the time whittling with Scout's knife. She carved little animals and little inventions out of the trader's small stack of snakewood, some of which seemed quite ingenious, at least to her.

They'd reached the bay, which rested on the edge of her map memory; she'd only sketched in points east. Chloe envisioned a road that led to the palace, a road reached from the far side, but the harder she tried to picture it, the more it eluded her. Not that it would matter. If Qujan was correct — if Chloe had written a world hundreds or thousands of years in the past — what good would her knowledge be? For the second time since Nick had ventured off, she felt completely alone.

Nob sat down beside her.

"Are we near?" Chloe focused on shaving a thin slice of wood from her block.

"Perhaps a day out," Nob answered. "Which is good, given what lives beneath."

Chloe made another smooth cut.

"I'm sorry, lady, this whole adventure isn't what you expected, is it?"

"No." She smirked. "I thought my school year would go differently."

"Tell me about school."

"Well..." Chloe set down her piece of wood. "We leave home and cram into a yellow bus that takes us to a green building where we learn math and litera-ture and geography — "

"I don't suppose they teach about Retinya."

Chloe laughed and placed the knife on the deck. "No. Just real places. I mean, real to us ... er ... no, they don't."

"I wish you could have come before." Nob leaned back. "When Retinya was beautiful. When Blind Secholit walked the ground and everywhere you looked — Well, it was a time. The three of us were royalty, you know. We acted a lot more like Secholit back then." Nob sighed. "Hard to believe. Look at Zophira now. Look at me. We don't resemble him at all. Maybe Scout ..."

"Tell me about the man you saw in the wood elves' mirror."

Nob didn't answer, and Chloe waved off her question. "You don't need to — "

"We lived near Shadowton." Nob turned toward Scout, who grabbed and held tightly to his knife. Nob peeked over the ship's edge, took a breath, and peeked again. Chloe hadn't seen him nervous before.

"Scout and I have always been brothers — brothers from birth — though it's a fact we don't share much," Nob continued. "Even before we were forgotten. Before Dad changed.

"Secholit called Zophira from a different family. From a different land. I don't know where." He paused. "I fear she forgets who she has become. To forget is a dangerous thing."

Chloe paused. "Then remind *me*. What am I doing here?"

"Only you know, but I think you are leading the wildest rescue mission I can imagine. Vaepor's palace is well-prepared for an army's attack. It may not be so ready for a girl like you. Either way, your arrival, and what has happened since, means Secholit wants Retinya back."

"And that's why I'm here."

Nob raised his eyebrows. Chloe gazed down.

"Lady? Did I offend?"

"No. Nob, will you be honest with me?"

"Always, lady."

"Since I've come here, people have been calling me … Let me start over. Do you think, I mean, do you think I could be, maybe …" Her face flushed. "This is so not a big deal compared to saving a world, so it shouldn't matter, but it does, because in my life at home it does, and I'm totally embarrassed to ask, but … Do you think somebody, not you, it doesn't have to be you, because I don't want you to feel like you have to say this or that or … And I completely understand if you can't answer me, or don't want to answer me, or—"

"Yes, Chloe. You are very beautiful." Nob grinned. "Does that answer the question you didn't ask?"

Chloe bit her lip and looked away. She let the words wash over her. *Yes, Chloe. You are very beautiful.* She touched her scarred face, and a lightness filled her.

"Thank you, Nob, I—"

"Ship ahead! Cloud above!" Scout called, and Nob jumped to his feet.

"Slaver." Nob sat back down. "Sailing away from us, thank goodness. Probably left a day before we blew out of port." He glanced up. "It's the cloud that doesn't look right."

Chloe lowered herself into the bottom of the boat. "Do we need to catch up to that ship?"

"No." Nob smiled. "We'll slow down. They aren't interested in … us." His voice dropped. "They're turning. What would make them turn?"

Scout exhaled slowly and pointed beyond the ship. "That'd do it."

Three funnels descended from a puffy white cloud directly in front of the ship. As they struck water, three waterspouts sprung to violent life, dancing and skipping and forcing the slavers straight toward the smaller vessel.

"In the Safelands, the land was too arid for Vaepor to materialize. Here It has plenty of water from which to draw strength." Scout ran his fingers along his blade. "Can you identify the ship, brother?"

The hulking boat closed in, and Nob squinted into the sun. "River dwarfs. Greedy little things. If it comes to fightin', we could do worse."

"I just found worse." Scout slumped. "Behind us."

Another ship closed in fast. It bore the same markings but was even larger than the first.

Caught between two slave ships? Perfect!

"So what's the plan?" Chloe asked.

The brothers looked at each other, then away.

Thunk!

A grapple hook from the first boat landed near Chloe's feet. Scout dropped his knife and yanked Chloe back.

Thunk! Thunk! Two grapple hooks from the second boat landed in the aft. Nob lunged at them, but both pulled taut. The deck of the Calainian vessel creaked and groaned. Scout looked at Nob. "This is a strange end." He pointed to the sea. Vaepor's spouts sucked beneath the waterline, and the waves churned. They rocked the big ships mercilessly; the oncoming surge would easily capsize their small craft.

"They will either board us or pull us in two," Scout said. "And even if they fail, Vaepor will see us drowned."

As the two boys stared at each other, Chloe nibbled her lip.

"Chloe." Vaepor's voice was unmistakable. "I'm above you. I'm below you. I see you." A wave crashed into their mast and ripped the sail from the boom.

Scout and Nob dived into the bottom of the boat, and inside Chloe, fear gave way to anger. "Well, that's fine, because I see you back!" She stood up in the gale. "And we're just going to wait here?"

"Our options are somewhat limited, lady." Nob grunted and pounded at the grapple.

I'm so tired of hiding from this thing — from everything!

Chloe cupped her hands around her mouth. "All right then." She stepped up and balanced on the boat's edge.

"Stay out of the water!" Scout shouted. "You don't know who rules this bay or what lies — "

Splash! She dived and swam toward the first slave ship. *If I'm so important, and it's me everyone's after, fine. Nob and Scout have done nothing but guard me. It's my turn to protect them.*

Fifteen seconds passed underwater.

Ahead, a school of fish approached, and for an instant Chloe forgot her predicament and smiled at their choreographed dance.

Thirty seconds.

The first fish came into focus and Chloe squinted. It was no fish, but rather a river dwarf; make that an army of swimming river dwarfs with Tuftunder leading the school.

She dived deeper, swam harder, and swallowed. *I must be nearing a minute.* The dwarfs, who had at first pursued, now watched. Then scattered.

They're probably scared of Vaepor's waves. Or they're running out of air.

Chloe peered down.

A huge, scaly hand wrapped around her and pulled. Deeper she plummeted, then deeper still, until all light vanished from above. Her lungs burned and her lips parted.

She opened her eyes, surrounded by brilliant light.

"Dead. I'm dead."

"No."

"Where is this?"

"A place where I ask the questions." There was a pause. "You are in the Sea Shepherd's domain. Why did you come so close to me?"

Chloe sat up and blinked. She assumed the bottom of the bay would be cold and dark. But resting on the bed, the opposite was true. Warmth and light flooded around her and she sat, breathing in water as if it were pure oxygen.

I'm using water for air.

"Yes, you are."

"A person can't do that."

"No. But you are no ordinary person, Chloe Lundeen." The Sea Shepherd walked toward her. Rainbow fish swam about him and shells hung around his neck. Ribbons of multicolored coral flowed from his hair. He was a beautiful, terrible sight. "Tell me what brought you here."

She winced. "No. I mean, I was given a task."

"No?" Echoes shook the water and the rainbow fish scattered. "You intrude and tell me no? Who gave you an unspeakable task?"

"Secholit."

The fish paused and the Sea Shepherd hinted a grin.

"Blind Secholit has returned … The world is indeed changed." The Shepherd took a deep breath. "No, then I suppose you mustn't share. But perhaps you can tell me what is happening here?"

He pointed to a giant conch shell. It darkened then lightened and then turned clear. Two men appeared on the shell's face. They bailed frantically as huge waves swept over their battered craft.

"Nob! Oh, sweet Nob! And Scout. They're friends. They're helping me!"

"Hmm. It does not appear so." The Shepherd swiped at the shell and the image disappeared.

"You've got to help them!"

"I don't have to do anything, Chloe."

Chloe closed her eyes and squeezed her hair, like her dad did whenever an idea got the best of him. She jumped to her feet. "You — yes, you — have to help my friends. Without you they won't live!"

The rainbow fish scattered again.

"There are many things that have never been done in my domain, and you have just done several."

"Okay, sorry, but haven't you ever had friends who really needed help? Please."

The shepherd pointed to the shell once again. The first slave ship appeared, covered with wet river dwarfs clamoring up its side.

"That's Tuftunder and that's his crew." Chloe pointed. "Slavers."

"Slavers, you say. I must have startled them." A wry smile worked across his face.

Chloe thought. "Well, maybe it was you, but they're probably more afraid of Vaepor."

The Shepherd scoffed. "Afraid of a wispy cloud? In the bay, I alone require reverence."

"Oh, I hear you. I'm just saying that the dwarfs don't seem to think so."

"They don't. Then they will be taught." He glanced sideways at the shell. "Their ship carries an awfully small galley of slaves."

The Shepherd swept away the image, and the hold of the ship appeared. In the center, a young boy lay shackled by the hands to a pole.

I know that face . . .

"Nick!"

"You know this boy?"

"I've been looking for so long ... Please help him!"

"And this other boat?"

"Another slave ship. But I only need Nick and Nob and Scout."

"And why has Vaepor stirred my waters?"

"I think he wants me." Chloe quieted. "He's so cruel ... Help us —"

The Shepherd pointed toward the sky. "I care little about surface comings and goings. Vaepor draws from my strength, but I don't feel the loss.

"And as far as your friends, this is my domain, not yours. I do as I please. I take who I wish to take, and leave who I wish to leave." The Sea Shepherd blew a trail of bubbles toward the surface. "Your courage, Chloe, is great. Foolish anger is not. And so I will aid your friends. *Two* of your friends."

"What? What do you mean two?"

"Nick, Nob, Scout; two will survive this crossing." The Sea Shepherd turned and walked away. "And you may choose."

I see heartache ahead for you, Chloe.

Chloe stared at the shell. The small boat listed badly. Nob gripped the mast and held on tight to Scout, who bobbed in and out of the water. Chloe whipped around.

"Please," she cried. "I beg you, please! I'm sorry I was so demanding."

"The next name you say is mine for the taking. Or say none and save none."

She rubbed her hand over the shell. Her tears burned and floated away. "I can't. I can't choose."

The scene on the surface worsened. The tiny boat capsized. Scout thrust his crippled leg out of the water and toward the boat.

"Oh, Scout," Chloe whispered. "You can do it."

"Done!"

The giant fist grabbed Chloe and thrust her upward. She shot out of the water and landed with a splash beside the broken mast. Once her eyes adjusted to the surface, she stared as the scaly hand wrapped its fingers around Tuftunder's boat and yanked one hundred screaming dwarfs beneath the waterline.

Chloe swam toward Nob, who clung to a plank. "Chloe? Oh, lady! I thought — Lady, I lost Scout. I lost my brother. I couldn't hold on. It's my fault."

"No," Chloe cried. "It's mine. It's all mine."

A wild scream. She looked up in time to see Nick splash into the water. He sputtered and thrashed.

"Help me!"

Without hesitation Chloe swam to him, gripped

him beneath the arms, and wrestled him over the mast. "Nick, stop fighting. It's me."

He turned his head. "Chloe? You're not a look-alike? Tell me something only you would know."

She thought a moment. "Front row, far on the right."

Nick's body went limp and he leaned his head on her arm. "I didn't think I'd ever see you." Coughs racked his body. "What's happened to us?"

Chloe shook her head and wept.

Dwarf divers leaped from the second boat and swam hard for what remained of the skiff. Nob looked up. "It's okay. They're friends from inside the mountain. Awake again." Nob lowered his head until it rested on the plank. "Please, lady, have mercy and take your leave of me when we land. I told you that you'd be better off."

Chloe stared at Nob with her hard Grandpa Salvador stare. "No. Not without you. He said two would reach the far shore. I'm not leaving you again."

"Who said this?"

"In the boat." She puffed out air. *I'll have a lot of explaining to do.*

CHLOE, NICK, AND NOB agreed to wait with stories until they landed. Thoughts were painful enough, what agony words would bring. But Chloe's mind whirred with dread nonetheless. *How can I tell Nob I'm the reason he'll never see his brother again? Will he want to go on without his loyal Scout? And what should I tell Nick?* She couldn't help thinking the whole mess might have been averted had he not set off on his own.

Their ship came ashore in Shadowton, a city well named. Unlike Medahon, Shadowton had no walls. Nestled in the mouth of the valley of the eastern range, it lay protected by enormous mountains that hid the sun even in late afternoon.

Chloe stood on the dock staring up at the peaks,

which disappeared into the clouds. Nob stopped at her side. "We're very close now," Chloe whispered. "I feel a heaviness."

"Yes, lady, close to the City of Reckoning. To the pool. To Vaepor. Maybe to our end."

"I need you —" Chloe said. "I need you to like me even after I tell you what I did." She tried to look at him, this friend who came back for her, but she couldn't even come within inches of meeting his eyes.

I'm so ashamed. Dad, I know exactly how you feel.

Her knees buckled and she stumbled, sobbing, onto the dock. Slowly, she calmed herself, and patted her back pocket. Her triumphant picture was still there — the image was certainly washed out by the water and her actions — but it was Dad's weeping photo that haunted her. She thought of him walking out from the barn. She thought of the rusted trailer and Inky and the Connect-It-All, his wonder invention.

She thought of him looking the other way.

What would he see in your eyes, Chloe? Again, another's voice pounded in her head. This time she did not look for the speaker — she knew who he was. *Anger. Bitterness. What would he find in you?*

Chloe buried her head in her hands.

No, Secholit. Maybe not now. Maybe he'd see love.

Nob held her, and Chloe felt the warm, wet surface of his face. In the city of his lost father, Nob cried too.

"Okay, lady, I'm here. No matter what you did, I'm not leaving."

She leaned against Nob and glanced over to Nick, who stood a few yards off, seemingly oblivious to their sob session. He spun a slow circle, a frown working across his face.

"Shadowton. A big place, right?"

Nob wiped his tears with the heel of his hand. "The largest of the five great cities of Retinya."

Nick stopped rotating. "So there should be lots of people."

Chloe rose slowly. "Where are they?"

A few men and women scurried around the dock, but the city was largely deserted.

"They're gone. Joined the others on Pilgrimage two days ago," a burly sailor with a deep scar under his chin called from his ship.

"But you didn't go." Chloe reached for Nob's hand.

"I've been there plenty, miss." He clutched his stomach and winced. "I didn't feel up to the trip this year." He stared at Chloe and chuckled. "I'm surprised you aren't with them."

"I've never—" Nob kicked her. "We missed them, that's all."

"Get a move on, then." He tied his skiff to the dock and stepped toward them. "When you hear the drummin', you know you're close."

"What is everyone talking about?" Nick looked confused. "We shouldn't follow anything. Let's stay here. I mean, we have the place to ourselves."

"Spoken like a fearful lad." The sailor paused. "But this fear might serve you well." His boots thumped heavy on the dock, which creaked beneath his weight. "I don't know what the girl told you about the pool, but the dunk is a terrifying deed. You sink, and your very memories float away until you can't remember why you ever came. You want to jump out, but around you memories, like shadows, moan and swirl, and you don't dare twitch, and so you stay." He pointed at his head. "This water tries to steal it all. Fear and faint whispers are all I have left."

Again, the sailor winced, and his face darkened. "My advice? Stay away from the pool."

Chloe squeezed Nob's hand. His skin was ashen, and she followed his gaze back to the sailor.

"Grandpa Salvador?"

Grandpa stood where the sailor had been, his

kind face smiling, eyes a-twinkle. Chloe stepped forward. "How did … how did you get here?"

"Through the window, in the same way you did. I'm so pleased to have found you."

He shuffled forward until his knees gave out. He straightened and smiled. "I miss our walks." Both Nob and Chloe inched back.

"Who do you see?" Chloe whispered.

"My dad."

Chloe's hands felt clammy. "Grandpa, remember when you accidentally filled my dad's rear with buckshot?"

"Of course, my dear. Such a fool I was."

"Why'd you do it?"

He paused, smiled Grandpa's crooked grin, and reached out his arms. His shirt and hands were covered with blood. "Give your grandfather a hug."

"Run!" Chloe screamed. She grabbed Nob's sleeve and he broke from his trance. She hustled Nick off the dock and onto the wharf, and the three of them raced through the city with Salvador's shape close behind.

"Why are we running from a sailor?" Nick huffed.

Chloe shoved him into a carpentry shop and slammed the door. "It's a Senseri or worse. He wasn't a sailor to me!"

"Nonsense." Nick frowned. "What's a Senseri?"

Nob pulled them deeper into the stockroom, where they scrambled beneath a pile of lumber. Chloe gazed out through a crack and fought to quiet her heartbeat. The door creaked open and Salvador hobbled in. He gently shut the door behind him.

"Why do you run? You've never run from me before."

And with this last word, her body exploded into its huge dragon form. The shop was far too small to contain her; all four walls and the ceiling blew apart. She flapped her wings and blood oozed from her underbelly. Scout was right — the wound from his blade had not healed.

"This has gone on too long," she croaked. "The two children are summoned. Come, Nob, go your way. I have no interest in a former prince."

Chloe looked at Nob, who shook his head.

"All right," the creature said. "You've tied your fate to the others'."

"Will you promise not to hurt him?"

Chloe stared at herself, standing toe to talon, wondering how she'd ended up in front of this dragon. All she knew was she lost Scout. She would not rob Retinya of Nob.

The dragon reached its neck around Chloe, examining her from all sides. She fought to remain still, but an icy shiver worked across her body. Chloe always imagined that dragon breath would be hot, but this creature's nostrils spewed cold — sickly cold.

"I make no promises about Nob, but he's no longer a concern of mine." She wagged her giant head to and fro. "And where's his majesty?"

"I don't know who you're talking about! You have me! Take me, you stupid dragon."

"Temper, Chloe. Not without his majesty."

Nick rose, rough boards clattering to the ground around him. He raised his hands and shrugged. "It's what they call me. At first it felt weird, but I'm getting used to it." He turned to the dragon. "It's about time you came back. What was that ship thing about? I was chained to a post. I almost drowned!"

"Apologies." The dragon forced a bow.

Nob grabbed Chloe's arm and yanked. "Nick's not on our side. He's a slave to that darkness. Haven't you felt it?"

Chloe took a small step away from Nick. "You side with Vaepor?"

"Well, I guess you could say I *was* Vaepor. He told me what to say, I said it. It's not a bad job, really. Creepy things slither around his palace walls, but they didn't come too near my place. Chloe, you won't believe the things I've seen."

Chloe couldn't speak.

"It's okay," Nick walked toward the dragon, who snatched him up in a talon. Nick wriggled and gave her an almost mechanical smile. "You'll see how cool this is."

"No." The voice spiraled down from the sky. "She won't."

"Pindle!" Chloe screamed. He looked so small hovering above them, but his face was stern, and the large dragon trembled.

"Release the lad, Yizash. I saw you hatch. On that day I rejoiced, but now I weep. What have you become?"

Yizash threw Nick across the shop onto a crumbled, wooden heap. "I don't — I don't know you. I don't remember you. You're an old one. You're all trapped in the hollows. You've been there — "

"Too long." Pindle launched into the sky, screeched, and plummeted down. Yizash flapped once but barely left the ground before Pindle tucked and blasted through her wing. A roar went out from the injured dragon.

"You will never fly again, daughter."

Yizash shrieked and beat the air. Her tattered, leathery wing provided no lift, and she crashed to the ground, flailed, and tumbled out of sight, leaving a trail of black blood as she fled.

"What have you done?" Nick walked over to Pindle. "That was my ride home."

"Home?" Chloe raised her arms and let them flop. "This is all wrong. Why did you live with Vaepor? Why didn't he destroy you?" She paced and rubbed her head like Dad often did.

What does Nick have that Vaepor needs?

"A body. A form." She raised her finger toward the sky and kept pacing. "Vaepor has no form, so he frightens everyone. But what if you spoke for him? People wouldn't be scared of you. They'd think his orders were kind."

"You're talking like a fool," said Nick.

"But why you? I mean, any Senseri could speak for him. Why did he need *you*?"

"Have you seen the pool, Nick?" Nob approached, each step carefully placed.

"All this business about a pool … No, I haven't."

"So you've been to where Vaepor dwells, but he's not allowed you in his palace or near the pool?" Nob repeated.

"Well, I've never been inside the palace walls. I stayed in a beautiful private house nearby …" He turned to Chloe. "That doesn't really make sense, does it? They called me 'your highness' but they didn't let me see the palace."

"Because you were blind," she said, and slumped over. "And you would see what I can't. Scout told me. Your eyes could see what lurks around the pool. You might even have seen our way home. It needed you and at the same time It was afraid of you. Now that we've both survived the bay, It wants you because you and I are dangerous to It."

"True." Pindle hopped over to remnants of smoldering wing. "If Vaepor gave one of my children any spoken authority, they would not give it back."

Nick frowned. "Why is he afraid of you?"

Chloe stroked her scar. "I think because I'm no longer afraid of him."

"May I suggest we move?" Pindle said. "I came to give you word. Five more ships full of those loyal to Blind Secholit have crossed the bay and even now reach Port's End. The march on Vaepor's palace stronghold has begun."

"So everything's working out!" Chloe exclaimed.

"The Old Retinyans are many for a dinner party, but for a war, they are too few. Unless they are joined by forces of thousands, their bravery will fail."

"And where are you going to find the rest?" asked Nick.

"May I suggest that if Retinyans remember who they are, you will have freed such a force?"

Chloe brightened. "Oh, Pindle, that's our last task!"

Help them remember!

Chloe ran to him. "Pindle, how quickly can you set us back on the Pilgrimage path?"

"In less than a day, but why enter what you can't leave? You found Nick. There will be no turning off the road. Let me take you to Port's End. You may approach a different way."

"You heard Secholit. You know where I need to go. I need you to trust me," Chloe said.

Pindle looked at Nob, who shrugged. "The force is mine to lead, but so is Chloe. I made her a promise. I won't leave again."

The dragon lowered his wings. "Well, then, I suppose we could fly, but we cannot follow the road out of Shadowton. We'll cross Lake Lemont, and you can rejoin the pilgrims three days out from the City of Reckoning. From then on, you'll be on your own." He sighed. "But go with speed. When Yizash reaches Vaepor, It will know the residents of Hollow Mount are freed."

"Which is why they'll need lots of help."

Pindle bowed low. "On my back, Nob, but don't squeeze too tightly. The skin is not what it once was. Chloe, Nick, aged talons hurt, but there is no choice."

"But he's, but you're … you're so small!" Nick said.

Pindle's face twitched and he fired toward Nick, skimming his hair and knocking him onto his back. The old dragon circled upward, glided down, and squeezed the children around the waist. The talons dug deep. *He wasn't exaggerating.*

"Stop it! You're squeezing too tightly," Nick cried.

Chloe breathed deeply. She would have another scar.

For the first time, that didn't matter.

Far beneath them, the sound of drums beat on. "From where the road intersects the march, three more stops remain before you reach the City of Reckoning." Pindle circled lower. "I have flown above the palace. I have seen Vaepor's hosts. Unless the people remember, unless they unite against the enemy, there is no hope — Old Retinya's final battle will be magnificent, but very short. Nick, I do not know you as I know Chloe, but I believe in you."

Nick grimaced. Pindle swept down, dropped them among a thick crowd, and was gone.

Pilgrims' steady footsteps parted around them.

"What in the world is this?" Nick cried.

"Why are you staring about, children?" A woman leaned over and smiled at Chloe's scar. She turned her head and proudly revealed hers. "Just a few more days and all bad thoughts and dreams will again be gone."

Nick's eyes widened. "What is she talking about? Whatever it is sounds good to me."

"Get up." Chloe hauled him to his feet and Nob fell in behind. "I'll catch you up to speed."

Drums pounded on, and the next three days blurred together. The carnival atmosphere that had surrounded the beginning of the Pilgrimage had vanished. Balloons and vendors' booths no longer lined the path, and pilgrims chose somber words over song and dance.

Older faces most clearly showed the unease. Their faces showed they'd been on this road many times before, and even though most couldn't remember the terror that waited in the pool, somewhere deep inside there must have been a glimmer of recollection, untouched by the waters.

Children seemed to sense the worry and no longer ran or played. They were tired, their voices filled with whines and complaints.

The quiet time gave Nick and Chloe a chance to swap stories, an exchange they made in hushed tones, and only during daylight when noise masked their words.

"I was such an idiot," Nick said. "I should never have set off on my own. I should have known. When they put me on the river dwarfs' ship, I still had no clue."

Chloe squeezed his arm. "How did you end up there?"

"I'm not sure. Things were going so well. I'd wake up each morning and walk around my private grounds. Everything was beautiful. My garden, the palace walls rising in the distance, the sea ... Dari said it was the most beautiful place in Retinya."

"Dari?" Chloe asked.

"Yeah, he was kind of my personal servant. Vaepor wanted him to make me comfortable. We spent all our time together."

Chloe frowned. "From what I've seen, Vaepor's not usually too interested in showing hospitality."

"I agree it was odd." Nick shrugged. "Dari spent most of his time watching me. I'd almost say imitating. It got to be uncomfortable sometimes. He asked more and more questions, mostly about our world. And the more questions he asked, the more curious he became. He asked about Mom and Dad and what it feels like to be blind. He asked about school and you and how I got here, and then it happened."

Chloe peeked at Nob. He was doing a terrible job of eavesdropping.

"Dari showed up one morning and he *was* me — looks, voice, everything — except he was blind. It was scary, Chloe. Next thing I knew, the bleeding dragon flew me to a port, a group of river dwarfs took me aboard their ship, and you plucked me out of the water. Good thing too. They said they were going to offer me to *him* in exchange for safe passage."

"Wait." Nob placed his hand on Nick's shoulder. "Vaepor has a copy of you inside and out?"

Nick winced.

Chloe stared back at Nob. "It's bizarre, but is that a problem?"

"Many still carry a faint memory of Secholit. They remember he was blind. They won't follow anyone but Secholit." Nob's eyes grew, and Chloe took over.

"So to bring *all* of Retinya under Its control, Vaepor would need a mouthpiece that pleased the eye to draw the young ones, and also was backed by all Its power to entice the dark things in your land. But the mouthpiece would need to act blind in order to win the allegiance of those who remembered Blind Secholit. The one who taught Dari would need to know what blind looked like, felt like, acted like." Chloe slapped her forehead. "And he'd need to be from a different world, where Vaepor isn't feared. No wonder It used you!"

"Vaepor couldn't know if Nick would remain loyal, so he made a perfect copy, one that would forever be true to him." Nob pushed his hand through his hair. "Who would speak his words and convince all of Retinya that he is Blind Secholit returned." Nob squeezed Nick's shoulder. "You were no longer needed, friend. You were to die in the bay." He quieted. "Instead, I lost — "

"Nob," Chloe said. "There's something about that day I need to tell you — "

Chloe crashed into the woman in front of her.

"Watch your step, girl."

"We've arrived," whispered Nob. "The City of Reckoning."

The city was not nearly as large as Medahon or Shadowton. In fact, it hardly resembled a city. "Maybe a prison," Chloe would later say. "Something from the movie *Escape from Alcatraz*." A series of watchtower rooms sat upon its towering gray walls, and shadows moved back and forth within them.

"There's only one gate in and one gate out. Then it's north to the pool. For ill or gain, our adventure is almost over," Nob whispered.

"Why do we need to march through a city?" asked Nick. "What good does that do?"

Nob glanced around and leaned over. "The pool.

It's Vaepor's prize. Think of the city as a maze, a series of roads all leading to the same point. The city controls the flow of people to the pool. Well, that's what I've heard from Scout." He dropped his gaze. "I don't know. I've never been this far. I never thought I'd be here. Oh, Secholit, what have you done to me? I'm just a ferryman."

"No." Chloe kissed Nob on the cheek. "Much more than a ferryman. You're my guide."

"Still, Scout would know what to do," Nob muttered and pushed ahead.

"Hey, Chloe," Nick said in a soft voice, and grabbed her shoulder. "If there really is a pool, and this pool lets you forget all your pains, why wouldn't we? I mean, why not go in?"

Nick said it aloud — the thought Chloe'd been pushing down since she first heard of the pool from the elf chieftain. But the harder she pushed, the idea, like a submerged beach ball, popped up at the strangest times and floated in front of her, all colorful and desirable. *Why not forget the horrible times? Why not be free of the shadows that haunt me?*

There'd be no more name calling, no more mocking. Not everyone was like Nob or Qujan or Grandpa. Every time her dad had looked the other way, every time he had ignored her — it all could be washed away. She could look at her dad without the memories.

What could be wrong with that?

She nodded. "There's so much I want to wipe away. But look at these people. Do you want to be like them? Do you really want to forget *everything*? I watched Secholit bury someone's pain, without stealing all that was good. That must be the harder, better way, I guess. But I hear you, Nick. Something in me wants it too. I want it so badly—"

"Closer! Press in, varmints! Adults to the left, children to the right. Surrender your infants to the carriers!"

Chloe looked up and shook her head. A giant three stories tall stood atop the city wall, straddling the front gate through which the crowd squeezed.

"The Crier." Nob closed his eyes. "No turning back now."

"Why separate families?" Chloe frowned.

Nob looked at Chloe and gestured with his hand. "Haven't you put it together, lady? Do you think these are families? They've forgotten everything. That includes who belongs to whom."

Nick gulped. "So each year families are ... recreated?"

"Faster now." The giant leaned so far over, Chloe

smelled his breath. "Through the streets, report to an open inquisitor. Step lively. We've many to serve today."

A wave of people pressed Chloe forward, and past Nob's outstretched fingers. She lunged for Nick, caught his arm, and hung on.

"Stay together!" Nob yelled from behind. "Don't lose each other. I'll find — "

"Nob!" *I never told you about Scout!*

His face disappeared in the sea of pilgrims.

"Looks like we're back on our own." Nick swallowed hard. "Chloe, I don't want to remember what sick was like, or what blind was like. I wouldn't stay in long."

Chloe reached her hand behind his neck. "How would you know when to come out?"

They reached the gate. It was a sad scene, like the good-bye from *D-Day Farewell*. People wailed. Women wept and handed over their infants; husbands surrendered their wives. Brothers and sisters huddled together. But this scene wasn't in a British railway station — instead it played out beneath a counting, snarling giant.

"Fifty. That's enough for this group." The Crier leaned over and slapped Chloe's back, sending her tumbling through the gate. She turned. The giant crawled down and blocked the entrance.

Chloe turned to Nick and wiped sweat from her forehead. "I guess I'm number fifty."

They funneled forward onto a thin street, lined with crumbling gray buildings, each one identical to the one beside it. Chloe'd never seen such a depressing city, nor had she ever felt so watched. Eyes peered out from each window, and Chloe quickly placed her gaze back on the road.

Escorts.

Their path wound like a snake, and Chloe quickly lost all sense of direction.

"What are we doing again?" a girl whispered.

"I don't even know where we're going," another hissed.

"No." From the front of the pack, a boy of twelve shook his head and stopped. "No. I'm not going. My year was just fine, thank you very much." He whipped around. "If you jump in that pool, you'll forget your name! Did your parents tell you that?"

There was silence.

"Think of your friends. You won't remember them. They won't remember you. This little group right here, this is all we have. We're it." He looked left and right like a scared rabbit. "We turn, hide in one of these buildings, and wait for nightfall. Who's with me?"

Nobody flinched, and then from the back, a boy's hand slowly appeared above the group. And then another hand, followed by two more, until there were twenty kids in all. They hugged friends and relatives and pushed back through the small crowd, disappearing around a curve. Chloe stood and waited with the rest, her palms slick. Anxious glances spread through the group, and for a moment Chloe thought all of them would turn and race back out.

Then, from around the corner, a kid screamed. Just once, the brave boy screamed. And all was silent.

Chloe, Nick, and the rest quickly began to move again. Soon the street forked and forked again. At each split, arguments erupted. Half the kids went left and half the kids went right, and after countless twists and turns only Nick, Chloe, and a handful of girls remained. Three small kids huddled together, watched over by an older girl who looked to be around eight.

"From above, this city must look like it's covered with spaghetti," Nick said.

Chloe nodded and moved toward her youngest traveling companions. "What are your names?"

"I'm Gina, and this is Leesa and Falia. They're my sisters."

"Are you triplets?"

Gina shook her head, and Chloe saw the beginning of a mark on her neck.

"Do you remember any of it?" she asked. "Do you know what happens next?"

"I remember." The older child spoke so quietly, Chloe barely heard it. "I remember it all."

"How?" Chloe glanced around. She repeated the question, this time in a whisper.

The girl puffed out air. "I'm Mara. We will meet the Inquisitor, who will let us pass to the pool. I don't swim, so when I step in the water, I stay in the shallows. They always yell at me, 'Your head, you must dunk the head.' I finally bob under and when I do I hear a voice. Does that sound crazy?"

"Go on." Chloe said.

"The voice always says, 'You have no reason to be here. Stand up, child.'"

I wouldn't hear that. I have a life full of reasons.

"I'm not saying things are good, I think I just empty out on the way. My dad taught me how." It was her turn to whisper. "Have you ever heard of Secholit?"

"Once or twice." Chloe grinned.

"Dad says that's who I hear in the pool. My dad tells me stories of long ago when people remembered.

Then I get out and go my way. See? Eight times in" —
she craned her neck — "and not a mark."

"But what if a kid went through stuff and did
things they didn't want to think about?" Nick asked.

Mara shrugged. "There's a different way — "

"You have no idea what some people live with!"
Nick yelled. "You don't know what it's like to be in
a hospital and be told you're going to die within a
year and that you'll never see again. You don't know
what it's like to be alone, in the dark. And the seeing
darkness isn't as bad as the inside darkness, because
all you want is one friend!"

Nick crumpled into a heap on the street, sobs
shaking his body. Mara cried too.

"I'm sorry," she whispered. "I didn't mean to hurt
you."

Chloe bent down, sat beside Nick, and wrapped
him in her arms. "I could have been so much nicer to
you back home. I never knew all that, but it shouldn't
have mattered and — "

"Move, children." A cold wind blew from behind,
but Chloe saw nothing.

"My friend is hurting!" she yelled. "We'll move
when we're ready!"

"Move, children." The voice was louder.

Nick wiped away his tears, glanced back, and jumped up.

"Run!"

He grabbed Chloe's and Mara's hands and herded the little children forward.

"Nick, there's nothing there," Chloe sputtered.

"Winged snakes don't bother you a little?"

The young ones screamed. "It's all right," Chloe said. "It must not be a very big one if we can't see it."

Nick grabbed her ear and yanked it toward his mouth. "It fills up the entire street! It must've been following us the whole time."

Then she heard it — a long, low hiss. A few yards back, stones scraped off the wall and tumbled to the ground.

"Okay, now run!" Chloe yelled, and Nick took off.

Chloe stayed behind the others, urging them on until her legs burned and the strange chill no longer worked her spine. She slowed and took in deep breaths while she turned a corner. They'd reached the end of the road. She approached the others standing clumped near the wall of a dead-end alley. A small door was set into the brick, with Nick slumped against it.

The gray around them felt so heavy, Chloe could

hardly move. She stared at Nick. He looked so frail. Mom was right; he'd been through a lot, much more than she could imagine.

"Accident." Chloe said, and plunked down beside him.

"What are you talking about?"

"You asked me about my nickname when we were on the bus the first day of school. One of my dad's inventions snapped, chains flew across my face. I was eleven. I've been scarred ever since."

Nick grimaced and rubbed his head. "The kids were really harsh. I was really harsh. But now ..." Nick stared at her. "But when I see you, I don't even see the scar. Honest."

Chloe nodded and playfully slapped his arm. "Then you *are* still blind."

"We need to go through," Mara said. "Shield your eyes, because it gets brighter through the door."

Nick scooted to the side and Mara pushed until hinges creaked and light surrounded everything. They all fumbled for each other's hands and stepped out of the alley. The door promptly swung shut behind them.

Chloe spun around. There was no sign of the door or the city. They stood in a glade of tall grass dotted with wild flowers, and directly in front of them sat a dark silhouette bent over a desk. It beckoned them to step nearer.

"Far enough." It spoke with a voice that made Chloe want to clear her throat.

"Names, all of you."

Mara stepped forward. "Mara."

The man Chloe assumed must be the Inquisitor picked up a large pen then set it down. "You are a confident child."

"I am answering your question."

"Come close, Mara."

"Don't!" Nick hissed. "There's nobody at the desk!"

"What?" Chloe asked. "I see him."

"They're all around us, these shadows. It's like she has an escort. She's surrounded by them, and they're looking at her neck."

"You've not been to the pool before," the illusion behind the desk said in a grave voice.

"I have, it just didn't take. Now let me pass."

Chloe hung her head. She'd just met the bravest girl she'd probably ever know.

Mara didn't wait for a response, but walked past the desk and disappeared into a brilliant light.

The three younger kids broke free and ran. "Mara! Wait for us." They too disappeared into radiance.

"Convenient." The Inquisitor scribbled and looked up. He pushed back from his desk and stared at Nick.

"Foolish Senseri. The word was sent out long ago. We need no more imitations of that boy. We found Nick weeks ago. Dari's transformation is complete and Nick's been disposed of. You can return to the streets."

"Go with it," Chloe whispered.

"But I want to forget. Even an imitation can want that."

The Inquisitor shook his head and waved Nick forward, and then turned his gaze toward Chloe.

"Name."

"Chloe Lundeen, son of Ray Lundeen, the famous inventor."

"Come close, child."

Nick was right. She felt cold breath on her neck as she walked.

"I see you've been here before. You may pass."

Chloe nodded and walked into the light.

Chloe heard a crunch. The gravel road on which she walked was just like the roads back home. She relaxed and kicked a rock, and a smile tugged at her mouth. But something was missing. She jogged and joined the crowd moving ahead silently.

"Chloe!"

Sound! That's what's off. Frogs and crickets and horseflies—

Nick pushed over to her. All eyes fixed on him in the heavy, unnatural silence. It wasn't a quiet made to be broken. "We must be near this pool."

She raised her finger to her lips. Near the pool meant near the palace. Near the palace meant near the trapped memories, if the elf chieftain's hunch was to be trusted. Chloe had no idea how to get inside the palace doors or what to do once she was there, but this was her task, and no good would come from being stopped due to Nick's loud mouth.

On either side of the road, a beautiful garden filled with exotic plants and flowers stretched to the horizon.

"We could make a run for it," she whispered. "There's nothing holding us here. We could hide in the garden until tonight, then if we don't see Vaepor—"

"There is no garden."

Chloe frowned.

"The road, it's lined with hideous things. Most of them are black and gray, so they kind of blur together. Giant dogs, walking serpents, Craeguls. And those oozing Kadim. They're all here."

"The who? How do you know their names?"

"They bowed to me. Even I can see it now. Every army needs a leader, and not one that dissipates over a desert. It used me for all the reasons you know, and now It has Dari." Nick bowed his head. "I feel so dumb." He peeked up and mouthed, "I'm sorry."

"You couldn't have known," Chloe said, and paused. "How many gray things are there?"

"Thousands. There's no way that a few boatloads of Old Retinyans, whatever they are, could beat them. You'd need every Retinyan, in sound mind."

"That's what we're doing, Nick. Trying to recover their memories."

"I know. It's just … I would so like to get rid of mine."

Chloe squeezed his hand. "Remember Mara."

And then they were there.

The pool wasn't at all what Chloe had expected. No terrifying, mist-covered blackish water. No bubbling cauldron. This pool was beautiful — large and round, with a lovely cobblestone walkway stretching around it. Water danced in the sunlight, and seven beautiful poles surrounded the pool, each made of mountain stone that glowed the most perfect blue.

Stolen memories set the stones on fire. She glanced down at her pocket. Her stone remained dead gray.

Chloe turned to Nick. "Is it really so —"

"Beautiful? Yeah, it really is. It's hard to see how it could do any harm at — Ugh." He shielded his eyes. "Vaepor's here."

Chloe spun a slow circle. "Why can't I see It?"

"Look up. Floating over the water. It's a cloud as dark as tar."

"And around the pool?"

"Them."

"Describe everything."

Nick took a deep breath. "Kadim. Big, oozing worms. Think of huge silkworms with tusks like elephants and you're pretty close. They've stretched their ooze from pole to pole, and it forms a dripping fence. They wiggle their way across that slimy barrier." He strained his neck. "That gunk connects all the poles but two on the far side. That's the empty gap. I suppose we exit through there." He squinted. "And there's stuff stuck in the slime ..."

"Go on."

He shook his head, and Chloe elbowed him. Nick didn't flinch.

"Kids. They're trapped in that ooze. They probably got scared at the last minute and tried to bolt into the 'garden.'" Nick's eyes grew sad. "There he is. Remember that boy who turned around on the street? One of the Kadi just pried him free from the fence and pitched him — "

Water soaked Chloe's feet and Nick pointed down. "There! Didn't you see that splash?"

"No, I don't see any of this." Chloe looked everywhere, frantic. "I need your eyes."

"Okay, well, people get out of the pool, all dripping and shivering. They're herded between the two open poles ... Let me see where they're heading." He raised himself on his tiptoes. "Okay. They're walking toward ..."

"A castle? Or a palace?"

"Uh, yeah, there is a palace but — "

"But what?"

"They never let me see it. The walls around it are really high."

"Okay, walls." Chloe urged. "Is there a moat? Or a drawbridge? You're the only one who knows what it looks like, so I need a complete description."

"No, you don't." He paused. "You've, uh, seen it before." He swallowed hard. "It's Aldo's Movie Palace."

26

CHLOE COULDN'T SAY A WORD. Finally, she stammered, "My great-grandpa Aldo's theater is here?"

"Well, it's about fifty times larger, I'd guess, but there it is."

The thought sickened Chloe. The Palace had always been her place of safety. How could her refuge lock up something as important as memories? How could Aldo's Movie Palace become the spot where people ditched the truth and hid their pain ...

Chloe closed her eyes, and her stone shone bright, its blue joining the blue from the poles around her. *It's always been that way.* She turned her stone around in her hand. *That's where I hid my pain. That's one huge reason why I loved it there.* She glanced around, then whispered, "Time to come out, Chloe."

"Wait, Nick," she said. "How would — You never saw Aldo's in our world. What's on the top of the marquee?"

"A diamond."

"What color?"

"Blue. It's blue, and once everyone gets out of the pool they stagger into the parking lot and go inside."

"They're told where to live in that thing." Chloe turned and saw Mara standing beside her. The girl's eyebrows raised as she continued. "We sit in a big room where the lights go off, and Vaepor appears on the wall to tell us what city we'll report to. It's chaos. But eventually we're divided into families and sent off for another year." She sighed. "Me, I'll slowly start back to Shadowton, where my dad hides and waits for me."

Chloe peered down at Mara. "I don't think they'll see Vaepor on the screen this — "

"Please. Will the next group of fortunate souls step around the pool? As you can see, the water's clear and cool, just what you need after a long journey. Too long have I been gone from my palace. I, Secholit, promise never to leave you children alone again."

He sounds just like Nick!

Standing between the open poles *was* Nick. An

older, stronger, more confident version. He took a step forward with his walking stick and shifted the dark glasses that shielded his eyes.

"Please, step around. Inside the pool you'll find refreshment. And yes, the rumors you heard about the pool are true. I should know. I created it."

"Liar," Chloe seethed.

"Do you have painful memories?" he continued. "They will vanish. Stay in as long as you like. There's no hurry."

Chloe grabbed Nick's arm and they huddled together, walking across the cobblestones to the far side nearest the opening. Nick ducked his head the whole time.

"Is there any other way to the palace?" Chloe asked.

"No," he said quietly. "Ooze all around. Those elephant slugs are crawling behind our back, Vaepor is floating above, and Dari is standing between the open posts. There is no way out."

I need some help. I don't know what to do.

"Who comes my way?" Dari continued. His face then lit up in a far-too-cheery grin. "What a compliment to have you return." He pointed his stick at Nick. "Friends, I sense I have an admirer. Is Chloe here?" He wagged his head back and forth.

"You see me just fine, Dari," Chloe called.

"Dari. A strange name for me. Feel free to call me Secholit like the others."

You aren't him!

"Are you missing your world, Chloe?" Dari said. "No, because it was a painful place, was it not? Jump in, Little Miss Scarface."

Chloe waited. Waited for the sting and the burn of the name, but she felt nothing.

"And Nick, you can forget your illness. Forget the blindness. You will be free."

All around them, people stepped into the pool. Dari inched toward Chloe. "Think about your father. Never looking at you. Never caring for you. Scarface. Scarface. Poor little Scarface."

And then they appeared. One after another, standing side by side on the cobblestones around the pool's perimeter. Quill and all his family, looking intently at Chloe. Activity at the pool continued as if they were visible only to her, which, as Chloe guessed, was the case. Qujan stepped forward. "He called you a name, a hurtful name. Could it be that this lovely scar, while it did alter one aspect of your beauty, gave to you another type of beauty, an inner strength, one you never would have known without it?"

Chloe's mind cleared and she spun a slow circle, a smile fixed upon her face.

Yeah, that's possible. That's really possible!

"Dari, say it again," she said.

Dari straightened and cocked his head. "Scarface."

"And again. It has a nice ring." Chloe strode toward him. "Scarface. I wept for Scout like my father weeps for me." The thought of Dad in the Quints' photo album flashed through her mind. She dug out her picture. Beautiful. Triumphant. Scarred. No longer was she the only one on the photo. A background had filled in — a pool, and Qujan stood behind it.

I made the memory!

"Scarface is a beautiful name," Chloe said. "Call me that one more time."

She passed by Quill, paused, and laughed. "Nice of you all to come."

Quill bowed and stepped back to make room. Chloe reached Dari and glanced at his forehead. Sweat beaded and traced down his face.

"You're anxious." Chloe leaned forward and whispered, "I know who you are. You don't need those glasses, do you? Why don't we just forget them?"

She swiped them off his face and threw them into the pool. Dari dropped to his knees and began a frantic search. When he looked up, it was with an expression Chloe'd never seen on Nick's face.

Dari's eyes widened and he touched his cheeks. "I'm changing back, Vaepor! I can't hold Nick's appearance." He crawled backward. "I have nothing over her. Take her!"

The sky darkened and Vaepor billowed overhead. Spinning arms reached out of Its mass. "You just keep coming, Chloe Lundeen," he thundered. "No more!"

"Come on, Nick! Follow me!" Chloe shoved Dari into the pool and ran through the gate. The moment her foot crossed the threshold, Aldo's Palace appeared, huge and imposing. She turned while running, looking for her friend.

"I'm sorry, Chloe." Nick slumped, his head engulfed by Vaepor. "I do want to forget." Nick waded slowly into the pool.

Chloe froze. *Don't let him go. Don't ever let him go.*

Okay, Grandpa! You better be right.

She spun and leaped back through the gate. She dived up into Vaepor's chilly mass, piked down, and dropped into the pool. Beneath the surface, the water was inky black. No light from above reached her, and she floated, surrounded by hideous moans.

I'll never find him ... Wait! The stone!

She dug it out and thought of Dad. The stone lit up the darkness, revealing Nick, treading water. Shadows — Nick-shaped silhouettes — peeled off him as the pool stole his memories, his mind. Chloe bit back tears while the shadows swirled, and then, pulled by some underwater current, whisked into a culvert-like tunnel deep below the surface.

The tunnel echoed with the agony of pain-filled memories, and everyone underwater, Nick included, fought to swim away from it.

The last of Nick's shadows disappeared, followed by one that looked just like Chloe.

Oh, no you don't! Not my memories. I've been down here too long!

She powered deeper and glided into the tunnel, where she thrashed forward, unthinking, until the tube bent upward. With a final kick, Chloe thrust ahead and broke the surface.

"Wow," she gasped, and soon stood dripping and panting in a darkened room beside a smaller pool. She tried to focus, to fix her mind on anything, but each thought slipped out of reach.

Salvador. There's a name I know. But from where?

Other names slid through her brain: Scout, Nob, Mom, but each was so faint. She had no faces to connect them to. Chloe stared at her stone. Where had she gotten that? It dimmed, and she glanced around.

I know this room. More shadows climbed out of the pool. They clattered the wooden hangers dangling from a rod that stretched from one wall to the other.

"This is a coat room. But from where?" She stepped farther in and ducked beneath the rod. She managed one more step before she stumbled to her knees. The room stretched ahead for miles, and crowding against the walls on either side, to the very end of Chloe's view, stood shadows of black.

They turned toward Chloe, but aside from a faint splashing behind her, all was silent.

"Who are you?" Chloe yelled.

Her voice fell. "Who am I?" She rolled onto her back, stared at the ceiling, and stomped the floor in frustration.

"I can't remember! I can't remember!"

She felt a trembling and opened her eyes. A shadow leaned over her, its gray fingers reaching to prop up her head.

"I know your shape! Dad?" Chloe's eyes lit up. "Dad. Ray. My dad. Chloe's dad! I remember your shape. I remember your face." Her smile disappeared.

"But you're his memory. What memory would Dad want to lose?"

The shadow drew back.

Chloe touched her neck. "My accident?"

It lowered its head.

A picture of Scout clinging to a sinking ship slid into her mind, and Chloe nodded. "It's okay. I get it now. I know what accidents are like. I know what it's like to be ashamed."

Chloe rose to her feet, cupped her hands to her mouth, and hollered, "I'm Chloe Lundeen. Do any of you belong to me?"

Shadows sprung off the wall and raced toward her. They circled her, enveloped her, and her head spun. But the dizziness quickly faded. She smiled, and remembered. Her mountain stone blazed fire blue.

"I'm in Aldo's! This is the coat room of the Movie Palace!"

She looked at all the shadows that still filled the room. Dwarf-shaped and elf-shaped and human-shaped. "Okay, you're all in the coat room of Aldo's Movie Palace. Did you know that? And I'll tell you why you're here. Or at least why I think you're here. Aldo built this thing on land that's part bog. Bad idea. Anyway, the floor cracks and water pools in the coatroom. So that's the water part, got it?"

It was silent.

"Okay, well that's not so important. But the other thing about the coatroom that was a bad idea — there's no door handle on the inside. You're locked in. Not that a memory could do much with a door-knob anyway."

She watched more memories climb out of the pool.

"But have no fear. I just happen to be Chloe Lun-deen, daughter of humble Ray Lundeen, the great-est inventor in the world." She placed her hand over her chest and bowed. "And I often had to chase my cat Streak into this very room, and on occasion this door would lock behind me. Do you know what I would do?"

This is a quiet crowd.

"I'd use magnetism. That's right. Magnetism. In that corner, you'll find a magnet, one that's very thin. It was one of Dad's inventions; he threw it away after the accident."

Chloe pushed through shadows and retrieved the magnetic strip. "I rescued it, and found that it's so thin and so strong you can slide it between the two doors like this and ..."

Click. "The latch repels and the door pushes out. Voila!"

The coatroom door stood wide open. Shadows shifted but didn't leave.

"Listen," said Chloe. "I know you're here because you weren't wanted. But the ones who let you go really need you. Vaepor has taken over. Everything in Retinya will follow It unless you help them. Remind them what it feels like to be free, even if it hurts." Chloe stepped up to her dad's shadow. "Whatever world they live in."

Whoosh!

A wave of shadows blew the doors off their hinges.

Chloe covered her mouth. "Mom wouldn't be happy about that."

"Nick. Nick. Where would you be?"

Chloe tiptoed into the lobby and slowly pulled on the massive handles that led into the auditorium. A film played, but Chloe didn't dare step inside — not with those creaky doors.

Wait. I can check from the booth!

She raced around the corner to the door that led up to the projection room and climbed the oversized steps.

Chloe heard the familiar hum of the projector. She breathed deeply, slipped into the empty room, and scanned the audience.

"I realize it may be difficult to remember events right now," Dari spoke from the screen. "After you are reunited with your families — "

"Yeah, right," Chloe muttered.

" —and sent back to your cities, it will all come clear. But your unwanted memories will not accompany you. I've removed them forever!"

On screen, Dari spread his arms, and the audience cheered.

Chloe's teeth clenched. *No more!*

"Liar!" Chloe screamed. "You're all being fooled!" Chloe crawled onto the window ledge, tested the beam of light with her toe, and jumped inside it. It held, and she bolted toward the screen. Beneath her, in the auditorium, there was a frenzy of activity. Shadow memories crashed through the back doors and into the theater. They hovered and swirled. For an instant, everything was in chaos, and then the room fell still.

"Kirth! Is my son Kirth in this room?" a lone voice sounded from the back of the room.

"It's me, Dad! Where are we?"

"You're all in the palace!" Chloe yelled. "It does not belong to Vaepor. You all just stepped out of a pool that did not belong to Vaepor either. But with these two things, It stole your memories. You now can have them back, though, and you no longer need to follow that … thing. An army of Old Retinyans comes to fight for you. Join them!"

Chloe raced forward as men, women, and children poured out of the theater. She crashed into the screen; it flexed and gave and let her through. She blinked and stood in front of Dari.

"I did it. I did it! Show's over. You're not fooling anybody." Chloe gathered her breath. "I completed my task."

"You may have temporarily saved these fools, but their pain will bring them back. You've doomed yourself, Chloe. Vaepor will never let you leave Retinya." Dari threw his walking stick to the ground and pointed back toward the projection booth. The beam of light filled with thickening smoke. "Vaepor comes now." Dari inched back against a wall.

The shapeless creature billowed and rose up around them.

"I did everything you said," Dari said. "I could not hold the boy's appearance."

"No, Nick," Vaepor hissed. "You didn't do as I wished. You didn't die in the bay. I think you two have done quite enough."

"Wait! You think I'm Nick? I'm Dari! I can see!"

Vaepor reached tentacle-like arms around Dari's legs.

"Chloe, help me!" He clawed at the wall. "Make It stop!"

"Let him go, you fog!" Chloe screamed.

Vaepor enveloped Dari's waist, and the boy stopped shouting. He lunged for Chloe's arm and squeezed. "Quick, go now, before this —"

Fog enveloped him. Dari offered one shriek, and was gone.

"And now ..." Vaepor closed in around Chloe. "The girl who will not go away."

Chloe looked around frantically. She was in a small building, with just the one window.

A curtainless, glowing blue window.

She inched nearer. Out in the audience, only one person still sat: Nick. Front row, on the right.

"Good-bye," Vaepor said.

"Good-bye back." Chloe ran full speed toward the screen. It bowed, and she stretched out her arms and clasped Nick's shoulder. "Hold on! Please, take my hand!"

His fingers wrapped around her wrist and they flew backward into the movie screen, as if fired from a loaded spring.

She landed next to her friend at the base of the window. "Stand up, Nick! Through the window. We're so close to home!"

"I can't see it. I see a little red, a little green. Oh, Chloe, you'll have to lead me."

She grabbed his arm and they stumbled toward the window. Though she tried to be careful, Nick slammed into the sill several times before they toppled through, both landing in a field of grass. Chloe sat up and looked both ways. "I know this scene. We're back in the movie. This is *The Vapor*, scene five!"

From inside the shack, there came a roar.

They stood, and Chloe risked a glance back into the room. It crumbled all around Vaepor, and bright light pierced the cracks. Creatures of all kinds and shapes burst through the walls.

"The Old Retinyans have arrived!"

"What do you see?" Nick slumped down. Chloe put her hand on his shoulder. He reached up and squeezed. "Your turn to describe."

"The walls are all down. All the Old Retinyans are advancing on Vaepor. And men! Hundreds, maybe thousands, are fighting, swinging swords in the air. With all the wind, Vaepor's having a hard time forming. Groundspeaker roars, and mountains crumble and waterfalls gush and, oh, green spreads across Retinya. It's more beautiful than we ever imagined or saw or ... There's my Nob! He is leading a charge from on top of Flit's back. Pindle flies at his side, carrying a man who looks just like

… I recognize him from the elves' window. It's Nob's father, and he's in sound mind!

"Oh, and I see the black creatures you told me about. They're scattering and the men are chasing. Some of the creatures have reached the edge of the Unknown Forest. If only you could see this, Nick. The elf chieftain and his army just swung out from the forest and wrapped them up in vine … the trees yanked them high into the canopy." She squinted. "And far in the distance, blackness has reached the Safelands, but the Sands are making short work of them. Now, it's only Vaepor. But how can you destroy something without a form?

"Wait, there's a breeze. Do you feel it? Stand up!"

Nick did and his hair whipped around his head. "It smells sweet."

"It's him, Blind Secholit. He's standing in front of Vaepor and blowing. Vaepor's fog is breaking up and blowing out to sea." Chloe breathed deeply. "It's done. He really was the hero of the story, Nick."

Nick's hair flopped back down and his head drooped.

Thank you, Chloe.

The voice was clear and strong, and warmed her through.

"But there are things I should have done and said.

I never got to thank the Quints, or say good-bye to Qujan." Her voice fell. "Or tell Nob what happened."

You may yet get the chance.

The window shone a brilliant blue and Chloe shielded her eyes. When she looked up again, all sign of the light had disappeared, as had the window and the shack.

"We're almost there." She turned and stared out into the theater. "Nick, you won't believe who I see."

"Tell me it's not that Vaepor."

Chloe grinned and dropped into her most sinister voice. "No, it's Mr. Simonsen. Come on! Give me your hand!" They leaned their shoulders into the screen and pushed. The screen gave as before, and they broke back onto the beam of light. Chloe squeezed Nick's fingers as they walked, side-by-side, over the audience and back through the projection window of Aldo's Movie Palace.

"Chloe!" the crowd yelled. "What's taking so long?"

She stared around the room she knew so well, the room that no longer felt like home. Nick's screenplay spread over the floor. Hobo, soaking wet, gave a shake and pressed into Nick.

"Wake up, Chloe!" Mr. Simonsen hollered. "We didn't pay for half a movie!"

"What? Oh!" The movie's first reel was over. *The Vapor*, reel two, was ready to show with the flip of a switch. Chloe reached her hand forward, and then drew it back.

That's not going to happen.

Chloe poked out her head. "Due to technical difficulties, we can't show the remainder of the film. Please see my mom for a refund."

She turned and listened to the grumbles and the angry squeak of the door. "We did it, Nick. I can't believe we actually did it!"

"I don't feel so good, Chloe."

"I feel great! I mean, we made it, right? Nick, we made ... Nick?"

He tottered, steadied himself against the splicing table, and collapsed.

"Nick!"

Chloe dropped down beside him while Hobo licked his face. The door flew open.

"Two things. Number one. Why didn't you tell me about the broken coatroom door? And number two. Why am I handing back money to — " Mom fell to a knee. "Chloe, call an ambulance."

28

CHLOE STOOD BY HOBO and watched the ambulance scream out of the lot.

Mom rounded Chloe's shoulder with her arm. "Nick's mom just called. They'll meet Nick at Children's Hospital in St. Paul. They asked if you'd care for Hobo while they're away."

Chloe glanced down. "Sure. I could never leave Hobo." Chloe reached down and gave him a scratch. Hobo stared back with sad eyes. "It's true. I wouldn't leave you," Chloe whispered, but Hobo looked away.

Chloe frowned. "Mom, Hobo and I are going to walk home."

"Go ahead. I'll clean up here."

They started what Grandpa Salvador called a thinking walk, a slow meandering stroll that took its time.

Chloe grabbed hold of Hobo's harness. The dog fell in at her side. "I miss them, you know? Nob, Scout, Nick, Flit. Even Mara. They kind of felt like family." She reached the end of her long driveway. "Now for my real family. Why am I nervous to see them?"

Hobo pulled her forward, and Chloe soon reached the farmyard. It was just as if she'd never left. A gentle wind blew leaves from the trees, the Snake River rushed in the valley, and men hollered from inside the barn.

I wonder if Dad's shadow made it back.

She bit her lip, turned toward the barn doors, and flung them open. All voices stopped.

Dad scratched his chin and took a step. "What brings you out here, Sweetbean?"

Chloe beelined for her dad and his grounded gaze. Chloe bent down and stuck her face beneath his stare until he was forced to peek up.

"I missed you," Chloe whispered and squeezed him tight around the middle. He tensed, then relaxed, and placed his hand on her head. Wet drops splattered on her shoulder. "I really missed you, Dad."

Chloe couldn't remember how long she hugged him. She so wished that Dad would have said something back. But she knew healing rarely happens all at once.

With Nick, it didn't happen at all.

Nick returned from the hospital—Mom said there was nothing more the doctors could do. Chloe spent days at his bedside, talking about where they had been, what they had seen. For Chloe, the memories brought excitement, but it seemed to be the opposite for Nick. Though his sight had returned, Retinya had been a dark world for him. Chloe often wondered if she should have left him there, in the pool. *Would he be in a different place? A better place?*

"Chloe, I want you to finish the screenplay. Would you do that for me?" Nick rolled toward her and held out his hand. "And will you watch after Hobo? My parents don't get him like you do."

Chloe thought for a moment before reaching out to grasp Nick's fingers. "Finish it yourself. You saw Retinya like I did. When you're better, you can write it all—you don't need me for that anymore. And Hobo? We can talk about me watching him later."

"No, we can't," he whispered, and faced the wall. "Will you get my mom and dad?"

Chloe nodded and walked down the hall.

She never walked into his room again.

Mom told Chloe it had been coming for a long

time. That his death wasn't a surprise. For Chloe, that didn't change anything.

No wonder he wanted to stay. No wonder he wanted to forget.

• • •

Chloe sat with Hobo on her porch. "So yeah, Nick's parents went to Nick's grandpa's place for a bit. Looks like you'll be here another month."

The dog cocked his head.

"Nick was ill … you probably knew that, though, being his dog. And, well, we lost him." She started to cry. "Come here, boy. I could use a hug."

Hobo rose, looked up at Chloe, then turned and limped away.

"Crazy dog. Doesn't know how to do anything but limp and lead," Chloe whispered.

Limp and lead. Chloe wiped her eyes. *I knew someone else like that. No — that's not possible.*

A grin crossed her face.

"Hold on!" Chloe jumped off the porch and caught up with Hobo in the yard.

"You're not in Nick's world anymore. Until his parents come for you, you're in my world, and maybe *I* can help *you.*"

Chloe bent over and removed the dog's harness.

"There. No more duties. You guided him to the end. Now it's time for both of us to play."

Hobo stared.

"Play. You don't know how to do that, do you? Well, it's a dog thing."

Chloe frowned and folded her arms. "How to teach a dog to play ... " A squirrel scampered from the large oak toward the elm.

"See, now that would be something to chase. Like this." Chloe stood and took off after the squirrel. She reached the tree and barked up the elm's trunk. "That was a ton of fun." Hobo looked at her like she was crazy.

"Or this!" She flopped on her back and rolled. "Dogs do this all the time."

Hobo slowly lay down.

"Yeah! That's it." She faced Hobo, her head resting on folded arms.

"We're both free. Look at you. No harness. Look at me. I'm — I'm beautiful." Chloe winked. "Your brother said so." The supper bell rang. "Come on, boy. Let's run."

Chloe hopped up and took off. Hobo limped behind her. They jogged by Grandpa standing beside his trailer.

"Chloe, tell your mother I'll be right in."

She nodded, and then paused. "Grandpa, I think sometime we should share stories." Chloe nodded toward his newest painting, featuring a short, otherwordly girl. "Would you believe me if I told you that I've met her?" She slowly reached into her pocket and pulled out her mountain stone. Grandpa's eyes twinkled.

"Oh, did you?" He set down his brush, stepped forward, and bent over. "What an interesting rock. Wherever did you find it?"

She closed her fist around the stone until a blue glow seeped out the cracks of her fingers.

Grandpa turned and hobbled back to his trailer. He stared at the painting and sighed. "Did she look well?"

Chloe slipped her hand into her back pocket and removed the photo. She gazed down at it, and then handed it to Grandpa. He stared at the picture, clutching it with shaking hands, until his chin quivered.

"Would you like to keep it?" Chloe said, and Grandpa pressed it against his chest. "I'll take that as a yes." She lowered her voice to almost a whisper. "Why could I see her? Nobody else could."

But Grandpa was in a different place, a different time. Chloe smiled. "I'll just leave you two alone." She turned away.

"Chloe!"

She peeked over her shoulder.

"Keep your stone in a safe place." He broke into a wide Grandpa grin. "You never know."

"No." She peeked down at Hobo. "You never know."

We want to hear from you. Please send your comments about this book to us in care of zreview@zondervan.com. Thank you.